GOODBYE TO THE HILL

To Jennifer
Happy Birthday !
Lee Anne
May 91

Goodbye to the Hill

Lee Dunne

WOLFHOUND PRESS

Published 1986 by
WOLFHOUND PRESS,
68 Mountjoy Square,
Dublin 1.

First published 1965 by Hutchinson, London

British Library Cataloguing in Publication Data

Dunne, Lee
  Goodbye to the hill: novel
  I. Title
  823'.914 [F]   PR6054.U55/

ISBN 0 86327 161 8

Cover design: Jan de Fouw
Typesetting: Redsetter Ltd., Dublin
Printed by Richard Clay (The Chaucer Press) Ltd,
Bungay, Suffolk

For my wife Nuala
and
for my parents
Katy and Mick Dunne
with my love

1

MY MOTHER came to the hospital at Clonskea. I was going home after a dose of scarlet fever. She held me so tight I thought I'd break and she cried bitter tears that wet my face. I tried to tell her that I was coming home, that I wasn't going to die and go to Holy God in heaven. She sobbed something awful and she kissed my face. I cried too, then. When my mother suffered, my heart couldn't hold back.

It was a long way home to The Hill, and when we had to walk it I knew that Ma didn't have the bus fare. My legs were as weak as valve rubber but I kept my mouth shut. If she'd had any money we'd have been riding.

On the way down we went into the convent at Milltown. Ma held me with one hand. In the other she carried a half-gallon can. An old nun filled the can with soup and bits of meat and potatoes and my mother thanked her, and there was a lot of talk about the good God in his almighty glory, blessing you and yours. I hated the sight of the nun in her long robe or whatever it's called, but I gave her a smile that warmed her feet. I liked the look of the soup.

Ma cried a little all the way down the Sandford Road and she told me how unhappy she'd been and how glad she was to have me back again. Poor oul' Ma, she was still at it when we got to the lavatory in Ranelagh. I held her hand as tight as I could and I loved her more with every step that my rubbery legs took. I told her not to fret, that everything would be all right. She looked down at me and her large sad eyes gave a little smile. It was as if she believed everything I said and I smiled back and gave her hand a big squeeze. The year was 1938 and I was just over six years old.

Many people can remember things that happened to them when they were six. I know I can. I can also remember how I felt about things, and that day as we went into a kitchen, one bedroom, a scullery and a lavatory, I was glad to be out of the hospital and still a bit sad to be returning to the flats and The Hill.

The Hill was a scab, a sort of dry sore on the face of Dublin. The hospital was so nice and clean, even though the smell of all that disinfectant drove you mad. And there you knew that everything was in its place, which was a feeling I liked. In the house, as we called the flat, the comb was in with the spoons and the knives and the boot-polish brush, and you slept three to a bed and you had to wait your turn to go to the lavatory. I didn't like this. There was something else too, though I couldn't make up my mind what it was. A long time after I realised it was the sheets on the bed in the hospital. I liked the feeling of the sheets.

Nobody else in the house seemed to notice that I was home. Even then I thought that it didn't cost them a wink of sleep whether I lived or died. Believe it or not, that's exactly how I felt. On The Hill you learned early, and you were more likely to be told to go and shite by a four-year-old than you were by its mother.

By the age of ten you knew all about puddin' clubs and doses of the pox and you smiled sardonically, even though you didn't know that that's what you were doing, whenever anyone talked about Santy Claus and the Stork and all that rubbish. And when Joe Soap got married after seven Mass on a weekday you knew that his missus was going to spend her honeymoon in the labour ward at the Rotunda. That was how it was on The Hill—you learned fast whether you wanted to or not.

At that time I couldn't stand my oul' fella. He never had any money to give me and he was always stopping me doing things that I wanted to do. He didn't work much but he was out all the time trying for a job. Usually he was in an awful temper and shouting at Ma and he'd give you a clip in the ear if you got in his way. I used to think he had it real cushy. Ma fed us somehow, so why was he always sitting there as though he had the weight of the world on his shoulders? I couldn't understand him, then.

My brothers and my sister were just a bloody nuisance. They ate grub that I could have done with myself and they were always in the way, pushing me around and kicking me up the arse, and if it hadn't been for Roy Rogers and The Sons of the Pioneers I don't know what I'd have done.

Somehow, Mondays and Thursdays, I got the money for The Prinner. Over the door were the words 'The Princess Cinema' and for a shilling you could have the best seat in the house, and for sixpence if you were a kid. The cheaper seats were eightpence for adults and fourpence for kids. Myself, I always went to the fourpenny rush. If I was ever lucky enough to have a tanner, I'd buy twopence worth of broken biscuits and munch my way through the 'folly an' upper'. I saw *Flash Gordon* and *Captain Marvel* so many times that I knew most of the dialogue off by heart.

After 'Hopalong Cassidy' faded, Roy Rogers was 'The King of the Cowboys' and Trigger was 'The Smartest Horse in the Movies'. I knew that this was right. It said so on the screen just before the picture started.

I was crazy about Roy Rogers even though he did sing sometimes. He was no Buck Jones; how I cried when he was burned to death; but he left Gene Autry standing. Honest to God, Gene Autry used to drive me out to the bog. You just couldn't take him seriously. I mean, he sang through his nose.

With Roy it was different. He could knock out six crukes

and not even lose his hat. And in the last ten minutes he always got hit on the head with a bottle or something. Every kid in the picture house would be hoarse from yelling at him to look out for the fella behind him.

'Roy! He's behind you! Jeysus, look out!'

'Duck, Roy! Mind your head,' and so on.

But he never seemed to hear and he got a right belt on the head and fell on the floor. Then the crukes tied him up and went off to rob the stage. Roy would wake up in about twenty seconds and he'd give a whistle and good old Trigger, the smartest bloody horse in the movies, would answer his whistle and kick the shack down. Then he'd untie the knots with his big teeth and Roy'd jump into the saddle and he'd be off like the clappers, firing two hundred and forty-nine shots out of his six-gun.

After a good gallop he'd come across 'The Sons of the Pioneers', who just happened to be riding by, singing their latest number. 'Cool Water' was a good one; written by Bob Nolan, the fella with the big chest; and when it was finished they'd all go after the crukes. There'd be a terrific fight and the head cruke would jump on his horse to make his getaway. Roy would see this and leap from the top of a rocky ledge straight into Trigger's saddle and then the chase was on. And the Lord help the villain when Roy caught him. It was usually a fella called Roy Barcroft that played the part, and God help him he got knocked out more times by 'The King of the Cowboys' than my grannie did by her second husband. And I loved every second of it.

Not only was I in the saddle every foot of the way with Roy Rogers. In the week that followed, myself and the other kids would relive the whole thing forty-two times, and whoever had the boxcart would be 'the chap'.

'The chap' was the hero, Roy. A boxcart was what it sounded like, an orange or lemon box on top of an axle and two wheels.

These normally came off some poor oul' one's pram, and with two bits of wood for shafts, the stagecoach was ready to roll.

'Listen, yis all can't be cowboys. Some of yis has to be fuckin' Indians.'

This was always the problem, everybody wanted to be the chap. The chap chased the stage down the lane and stopped the runaway horses. The chap went for his gun; his hand came up like a flash from his hip, first two fingers forward, the thumb cocked, last two fingers folded against the palm like the butt of a gun; and he outdrew the villain every time. This was no accident, there had to be some kind of production bit.

'I'll be the chap and you must be the cruke and you must go for your gun and I must beat you to the draw.'

The poor oul' villain, he never had a chance. Anyway, I stuck with being an Indian or one of the crukes until I was about eight. Then I realised that the fellas who got shot in the earlier part of the picture weren't very important. If you couldn't be Roy then the head cruke was favourite.

In the end I got myself a really strong box, stole an axle and a thick pair of iron wheels and I paid one and sixpence for the best pair of shafts ever seen on The Hill. I had the boxcart to beat them all and from then on I was always the chap. I shot more Indians and outlaws than all the cowboys in Hollywood put together, and inside my funny little mind I was certain about one thing, I was never going to be an Indian again.

The boxcart earned its keep too. I used it to carry sacks of turf for old women who were on their last legs. This was usually worth a deuce or even threepence and once I did so well that I took my little brother Larry to The Prinner on the strength of one's days work. That was a bad mistake.

Larry yelled and cried every time a car or a train came towards us on the screen and I had to keep belting him on the head with a lump of sponge that I'd torn out of the arm of the seat. It didn't stop him crying, but I kept doing it anyway.

An oul' one sitting behind us in her eightpenny seat started complaining, and the gunner-eyed attendant came up and dragged us out. He took the sponge off me and gave me a belt in the face with it. I gave him a kick in the shin, but it didn't hurt him much on account of me having no shoes on and he gave me another few belts with the sponge and threw us both out on the street.

I was going to give Larry a good kicking till I saw how upset he was. So I told him to shut up even though he wasn't saying anything, and I took him home. Ma had to give him a bath that night and she had a terrible job cleaning his trousers. As you might well imagine, I didn't take him any more.

As well as going to school I was working too. Before and after school I did two paper rounds and I was pulling in five and tenpence a week. I used to give Ma the dollar and it was a gift to see some of the worry go out of her face when I put it in her hand. Mind you, I hated them effin' paper rounds. They shagged up my chances of playing football after school, and if there was one thing I loved it was football. Still, there was the odd bit of compensation. The early morning is a good time for nicking things.

In the summer I got more than my share of apples and pears and I used to flog them for three and four a penny on the way to school. Many's the tree I stripped to get my picture money. You see, most of the kids were forever hungry so that anything you could eat was always a quick seller. Sometimes I used to give two or three to a fella to do my sums for me. We were doing long division in class now and I just couldn't get the hang of it. When I added three and three and got six I was delighted with myself, but that was as far as it went.

Also, on Fridays and Saturdays a lot of the people on the paper rounds used to leave out the money for the milkman, and though there were quite a few kids at it I used to get the odd few bob that way. I didn't take any chances, though. If you got caught you could be sent to a reformatory school, and I heard from a kid that was in one that they were bloody awful places to be sent to.

I didn't mind the winter either, because I never suffered from the cold once I was on the move. Sometimes, lying in bed I felt cold and often wished we had a few more coats to throw over us. But running along in the rain or even the snow was okay. Even the bad winter when I had no shoes didn't bother me. I ended up with the toughest pair of feet in the flats and none of the other kids could touch me when we raced across the stones.

This was a square half-acre of ground that was all stones and gravel and the kids used to play football on it. Some of the flats faced on to it and the oul' ones were for ever coming out and screaming about their windows getting smashed. Nobody minded them very much; football, along with religion and poverty, was about the one thing that the kids had in common.

One day when it was snowing hard I kidded Ma that I was too cold to go to school. She sent a message down to the master and he sent back word that I would get a voucher for a pair of boots if I went to school. These were a charity issue and they had a stamp on the soles to stop them ending up in the pawn office. But still some of the oul' ones managed it by burning off the stamp with a red-hot poker and getting Maggie Flood to take them down at lunchtime.

That was the best time, because the young apprentice was usually on his own and he'd do anything for Maggie. She'd be in the pawn office for ages and one day, when another kid and myself followed her down and tried the door, it was locked. The oul' ones used to smile among themselves and I heard two of them talking when I was above in the dispensary waiting to see the doctor. They said it was the size of her tits that did it with the apprentice, but I couldn't understand what they meant. To me, Maggie Flood looked just like a big cow.

13

Anyway, I never got the boots and I was glad about that. They were black ugly things and you could tell by looking at them that they were for nothing. Ma was angry with the master for not keeping his promise, but I thought he was all right. And, anyway, I loved running about in my bare feet.

2

THERE was a right load of young ones living in the flats, but I didn't like any of them very much. They were all snotty-nosed and as common as ditch-water, and when I saw some of the young fellas trying to kiss them an' all I used to wonder how they could do it.

All the times I'd seen Buck Jones, and Tom Mix and Hopalong Cassidy, Roy Rogers, Ken Maynard and Charles Starrett, The Durango Kid—

> In days of old when men were bold
> And the bandits ran the skid
> Out of the hills came a daring young man
> They called him The Durango Kid.

I'd never seen one of them kiss the mot. They got her away from the outlaws all right, but in the end they always rode off on their own. Jeysus, I used to love it when they turned round in the saddle and waved goodbye, just before they went over the hill, into the next adventure. So I couldn't understand fellas who chased snotty-nosed mots and tried to give them a kiss and all the rest of it. I thought it was much better to play 'Rough Riders' or 'Gang Busters', but one day, when I was below in the shop waiting for the papers, Janet Blair changed all that.

I was nearly thirteen and I was the quickest draw in the flats and I felt smashing then, having just learned to ride a bicycle. This was really something; there weren't many kids on The Hill who could ride a bike.

This particular bike belonged to a fella who was going with a girl from the flats. You'd see him waiting until her mother and father had gone down to devotions in Rathmines Church, then he'd slither into the house like a fella in an awful hurry. I don't know what him and the mot used to get up to, but he was never in a rush to come out again, so I started to take a loan of the bike.

I couldn't sit up on the saddle, so I used to stick one leg under the crossbar and ride it like a monkey. It was great gas, with me imagining that I was Roy Rogers on Trigger, galloping after the outlaws. Once or twice I got a puncture; there was always a load of glass lying about on the streets; and I just pushed the the bike back and left it where I'd found it. Then one day when your man went in he put a padlock on it and that really annoyed me. I was so used to having a ride by now that I just knew I'd have to get a bike of my own. That was my first dream.

The oul' one was awful slow marking the papers and I saw Janet Blair on the cover of this magazine. She was in a bathing costume like I'd never seen before and I lost my breath when I thought how beautiful she was. Her chest seemed swollen too but it wasn't like a cow's like Maggie Flood's. It looked all soft and nice and clean and when I touched her there on the cover, I swear to God, I got a thrill that nearly killed me.

I swiped the magazine before I left and I looked at her picture every foot of the way on the paper round. Even when I put the magazine in my pocket I could still see her lovely face and the shape of her, and that was the first time I ever loved another woman except my mother.

After that day I more or less stopped going to 'The Prinner'. It was no good going; all the time I wanted Roy and the others to start kissing the mot; all they ever kissed was the horse; so I began going regularly to The Stella.

This was another picture house further up Rathmines Road, and the best seat in the house cost about one and eightpence. They got a different type of picture there, with only the odd cowboy thrown in. I began to see Clark Gable and Charles Bickford and George Murphy and lots of others, and there was always a terrific mot in the story.

Now, to see the hero trying to kiss the girl every chance he got seemed to me to be smashing. And if Janet Blair was on I used to work and steal or do anything to get the money to go every night. I would have married that girl if I'd had the chance.

When Ma found the magazine in my coat she gave me a right-hander across the face and said she was going to tear it up. It was old and torn by now; I'd had it the best part of six months; but I asked her not to do it. She looked at me in a strange sort of way and then without another word she handed it back to me. Then she hugged and me held on to me for a minute. When she looked at me again I had the feeling that I didn't look the same to her any more.

'It's little wonder yer old before yer time,' she said. Then, smiling suddenly, she growled at me, 'Yer father'll kill you if he sees it.'

'Don't worry, Ma, he won't,' I said, 'and thanks, Ma.'

I tore up the old magazine, but I kept the picture of Janet in my pocket, and when it got badly worn from being folded and unfolded I got some sticky paper from the post office and stuck it together at the back. Finally, another kid nicked it off me, but I couldn't prove it, so that was the end of it. Not that it really mattered, because by then I was starting to put into practice all the things I'd been thinking about for so long.

Mrs. Kearney was the beginning, I suppose, but I'm not blaming her. It was bound to have happened, anyway, before very long. She just made it a lot easier than running after the young ones who lived on The Hill.

I was over fourteen and I was tall, even though I was only as broad in the chest as a kipper. I still did the paper rounds and I worked as much as I could with the boxcart. It served no longer as a stagecoach. Now it was strictly a commercial vehicle, and I tended to several gardens at two bob a lawn. I also cleaned windows and washed the odd motor-car and on Saturdays I did a full day's work in a butcher's shop for five shillings.

This was fantastic money for one day, but as I had to work from eight until eight you can imagine the state I was in, with the papers to be delivered as well. Pushing the carrier bike around, with all those Sunday dinners in the basket, was hard work, but I loved to ride the bike so much that I didn't care. And Jimmy the butcher was a decent skin. He always gave me a wrap up when I finished, which meant that we had a good stew at home on a Sunday with all the bits of meat he'd had left over.

For the afternoon paper round I used to get a couple of kids to help me and I'd give them a deuce apiece for doing most of the work. I'd flash down to the shop on the bike, pick up the bundle of papers and then split it with the kids. I'd do as many as I could on the way back to the shop, leaving them to clear up the rest. Then back to the butcher's like a rocket. I'd tell Jimmy I'd been to the bog or something and he never once said a word. He didn't care as long as I got all the meat delivered.

It was a joint of roast beef that took me to Mrs. Kearney's. I hadn't seen her before, but I'd heard Jimmy and the apprentice Slattery talking about her. I was pickling a bit of beef and I think they must have forgotten that I was in the shop.

'She likes good meat, that Mrs. Kearney,' Slattery said.

'Yer right there, boy,' Jimmy laughed. 'There's not a woman in Rathgar who's more fond of good meat than Mrs. Kearney.'

He grinned at Slattery. 'That's how she got them big headlamps and them lovely child-bearing hips,' and he laughed again as though somebody was tickling him.

Poor Slattery smiled all shy at that. He was from the bogs and he was as green as a head of cabbage with his freckled face and a head on him like a turnip. You just couldn't help feeling sorry for him.

Mrs. Kearney herself opened the door when I got there with the meat, and the minute I saw her I knew what Jimmy had been talking about when he said headlamps. God, they were nearly bursting through the wool of her jumper and I got such a start that I nearly dropped the meat on the doorstep.

She had big teeth like a horse, but she was a fairly good-looking woman, even if she did wear glasses. I couldn't take my eyes off her swollen red jersey and I was shaking something terrible as I handed her the meat. There was a hot sting in my bowels too and I was thinking that I'd do it in my trousers if I wasn't careful.

'What's your name?' The way she said 'your' made it sound as though my name, whatever it might be, was going to be very important to her. I was still shaking with nerves, but I had a feeling that there was a chance with this woman. I'd heard all the bigger fellas on The Hill talking about all the things they did with women and, afraid or not, I was itching to do something. The fact that Mrs. Kearney was probably old enough to be my mother didn't make any difference to me.

'Maguire, ma'am. Paddy Maguire from Rathmines.'

'There's a good lad.' She smiled at me full blast. 'Would you care for a cup of tea?'

Now, if there was one thing I never did it was drink tea. Ma always kept a packet of cocoa in the house for me, and even when I'd gone to Balbriggan with the boys' club I'd taken my own packet of cocoa and I'd drank nothing else for the whole week's holiday. I just couldn't put tea down without the feeling that it was going to come straight back up again.

'I'd love a cup, ma'am, please,' I said, and nothing was further from my mind than cocoa.

'Come in, then,' she said; 'come in and I'll stick the kettle on.'

The house smelled nice and the kitchen seemed as big as our whole flat. It was all spotlessly clean. The paintwork was all new-looking and even the lino on the floors was shining good enough for you to see your face in. I liked it very much.

She put the kettle on the gas stove and I sat down. She stretched up to put the meat in a wall cupboard and her skirt went up her legs a bit and I was warm all over. She turned round then and looked at me.

'What job are you going to do when you're older, Paddy?'

'A landscape designer, ma'am,' I said, thinking of one of the gardens that I looked after in Cowper Road. I didn't mean it for one minute but I thought it would sound better than a bus driver or the like.

'And a lady-killer too, I'll bet,' she said, smiling. 'You're a very good-looking young man.'

I didn't know what to say to that. I was very nervous, so nervous that it wouldn't be easy to talk at all, let alone make this kind of chat. Suppose I was kidding myself, anyway, that the woman was just giving me a cup of tea. I'd be in right trouble and Ma would be bound to hear of it. It might be as well to get up and go. God, look at her chest, so big and so round, and my trousers getting tighter every minute.

'You're shy, Paddy. Sorry, I didn't mean to make you shy.'

'Oh, you didn't, ma'am, you didn't at all. I'm a bit worried about the bike, that's all.'

'Oh, is that all? Oh, don't worry about that. It's perfectly safe out there.'

When she poured out the tea I took a mouthful, hoping that it would help me relax a little. The minute it hit the inside of my mouth I wanted to throw up.

'Excuse me, ma'am, may I use your toilet, please?'

'Of course, Paddy. It's upstairs. I'll show you where.'

I walked behind her up the stairs and it was though she had a big pendulum in her skirt. God, it was agony to watch. She opened the bathroom door and when I went in she followed.

'It's all in the one,' she said, indicating the bath and the lavatory pan. I stood there, but she didn't make any move to go out. She bent over the bath and began to put some clothes that were lying in it into a bundle. I didn't move. I just stood there waiting for her to go, knowing at the same time that she wasn't going to. There was excitement and fear running through me. I knew something was going to happen, I could feel it. I also knew that I wasn't going to be sick and I couldn't have taken a piss to save my life.

She straightened up from the bath and taking me by the arm she drew me against her. I was hypnotised, and even if I'd wanted to I couldn't have stopped her from pulling me close. She put her arms around me and she kissed me on the mouth, pulling me hard against her body, and I came, fiercely upon myself, for the first time in my life.

I shook from it and she must have known, for suddenly her arms were cuddling me and she was different to the way she'd been, only seconds before. She pressed my face gently against her breasts and it's impossible to describe the feeling that I knew. I thought for a second that I was going to cry, but I held back. No woman except Ma had ever seen me do that. I had to get out of there and I felt that she understood that too. She was kind to me, and anyway she probably knew that I'd be back again before very long.

There was a change in me from that moment in the bathroom. It's a hard thing to explain. I didn't look any older, yet I could feel the change, almost as if I'd never be a kid again. It was like turning a bend in the road. Something is behind you, but it isn't there any more and you're different because of that.

There were fellas on The Hill who claimed that they'd been

in bed with women lots of times, but they still looked the same to me. They didn't even sound different or act at all strange, so why should I feel odd after what had happened? I couldn't figure it out at all, I just knew that I would never be the same again.

3

THINGS were happening all the time on The Hill. Babies were being born to people who couldn't afford to keep themselves. Old people were dying, most of them in poverty and loneliness from which death could only be a welcome release. And all over the place governments were coming and going like snuff at a wake and people were saying that this would happen and that would happen now that the war was over.

None of this mattered to me; the war hadn't cost me a thought; as far as I was concerned 1945 was just another year; I was getting hard, becoming immune to the sight of snotty-nosed half-starved kids growing up in filth and squalor, so that the endless arrivals, the new screaming bundles, didn't depress me. I'd seen, too, the old wagon take away enough paupers to enough quick-lime burials to be used to that as well. Most of the poor oul' bastards had never had the chance to live, anyway, meandering through a pointless grey existence, unrelieved by the least shot of colour. Death might be something new.

Governments and politicians were just words and pictures in the newspapers that I delivered but never read. Voices from tall platforms making promises that they had no intention of keeping. Strangers in good suits and white linen, pleading for the trust of other strangers, talking to them like friends but making sure by the very promises that they weren't going to keep that strangers they would always be. Catholic and Protestant alike, on the common ground of the platform, sharing only an abhorrence of poverty, contempt for the helpless fools that were drowning in it and the ability to tell lies, while managing to look and sound as though they believed every word of what they were saying.

I suppose I hated them. They were only bloody vultures, just helping themselves to anything that they could lay hands on. But if I hated them I didn't really blame them. Anyone else, given half a chance, would do exactly the same thing.

I listened to what they said. I listened to everybody and I enjoyed doing it. I loved to get people talking about themselves. It didn't matter to me who they were or what they did. Everyone had a story to tell and I lapped up every word. I was like a big sheet of blotting paper, just walking around soaking up everything.

Each week now I did a few jobs for Mrs. Kearney. I looked after the garden and I cleaned the windows and she paid me well. You could tell she wasn't stuck for a few shillings and with what she gave me, and all my other numbers, and the paper rounds and the butcher's on a Saturday, I was earning a nice few bob, even though I didn't have a steady job.

Mrs. Kearney kissed me every chance she got and though I thought it clever to be doing it, I didn't think it was all that it was cracked up to be. I mean, when those blokes on the screen in The Stella kissed the mot they looked like they were in heaven. I wondered a few times if it would have been any different if I'd been doing it with Janet Blair or Betty Grable. Then I had a chat with Harry Redmond and he soon made me realise that I wasn't putting enough into it to get much out of it.

Harry Redmond was a layabout and a tired layabout at that. He'd never been known to do a day's work in his life, and though he was thirty-six years old his mother still regarded him as her little boy Harry.

Anyway, as I say, Harry passed the time without ever having to take a job to relieve the boredom. He did go down to the Labour Exchange several days a week to put his name on the line and he always bussed it back home on payday. And when people asked him what he did he used to tell them that he was an artist, though you can take my word for it the only thing he ever drew in his life was the dole.

I bumped into him one day as he was coming out of the reading room at the library. He was in the mood for a chat, so we sat down on a seat at the bottom of Leinster Road and he began to talk about women. Or, to be more truthful, he began by telling me about horses. The mare had to be serviced by the stallion. This operation produced little horses that were called foals. I knew this already, but I didn't want to hurt his feelings after him taking the trouble to tell me, so I kept my mouth shut.

After a while he got around to women and if there was any truth in what he said it wasn't any wonder that he was always so tired-looking. According to himself, there wasn't a scivvie in Rathmines that he hadn't flung one up, and that went for Rathgar and Terenure as well.

He didn't spare the details and with him being a born story-teller he had me so worked up that I'd have jumped a bus and gone up to do the grass for Mrs. Kearney, only I knew that she was up at the chest hospital visiting her husband.

When Redmond stopped for a minute to roll a cigarette I asked him a few questions. I was careful how I put them. I didn't want him to think I was pig ignorant altogether, even though that's exactly what I was. And to give him his due he did all he could to put me right.

'A woman gets the same kick out of it as a man does,' he said, running his tongue along the edge of the cigarette paper. 'That's why they love it so much.'

It made sense when you thought about it, but up to then I

hadn't done so. I'd taken it for granted that women only did it to please men or because they wanted babies. I just hadn't ever considered that they might have been doing it for pleasure.

'The whole secret is,' he scratched a match on his shiny trouser leg, 'to make sure they come at the same time as you do. If you don't do that you're wastin' your time.'

He told me how you could work this and I thought that he must have been an awful cool customer altogether to be able to think while he was doing it. The minute Mrs. Kearney touched me my head was full of little explosions and it took me all my time just to keep breathing. And he went on about using your tongue when you kiss women and how you should play with them when you were going to give them one. He said they all liked it if you played with them first. I drank in every word, all the time wishing that Mrs. Kearney wasn't above at the feckin' hospital.

By the time Harry got up off the seat to go home for his square meal as he called it, I felt very much the wiser. And when I went up to Mrs. Kearney next day I tried to keep in mind all he had said.

I felt the surprise in her when we kissed. For the first time I opened my mouth and I could feel the warm breath of her and I knew then what it was like to kiss and be kissed in return.

She took me to bed that day and though I hardly did the sheets any good at least I didn't want to cry after the first time. I wanted to stay there in the warm bed, with her arms wound tightly about me, and I did for the whole afternoon.

She seemed to be delighted with me and I enjoyed myself so much that I even forgot about Janet Blair for a while. When I finally left the house Mrs. Kearney gave me five shillings and I hadn't even cleaned the windows. When I walked down the road I was eight feet tall and all shiny and new and the two half-crowns felt like cartwheels in my pocket. I got a shock, though, when I saw the time and I knew I'd have to get a move on if I was going to get the papers delivered.

An empty taxi came cruising down the road. I put up my hand and he stopped with a look of surprise on his face. Not many people hailed cabs in Dublin.

'How much down to the Avenue?' I asked.

He seemed like a fairly nice oul' fella and he grinned at me with his clear gums.

'Two bob,' he said, trying it on.

'Ah,' I said, in my best poor mouth, 'I only have nine dee.'

He gave me an old-fashioned look, so I spoke up quickly.

'I was up seein' me grannie. She's dyin', ye see, and I stayed longer than I should've. I didn't like to leave her, ye see. Now I'm late for to do me paper round.'

'Ye' for 'you' and 'me' for 'my' deliberately stuck into the chat to try and make it sound poorer. He looked at me for a few seconds and then reaching over he opened the door.

'Jump in,' he said, 'I'll run you down for the nine dee.'

He put the car into gear and I'll say this for him, he got a move on for such a gummy oul' fella. He didn't say much, just kept chewing on his gums and spitting out of the window as if he had a filthy taste in his mouth. I asked him to stop before we got to the paper shop. It wouldn't do to let the oul' one see me getting out of a taxi. She might decide that I was nicking things that belonged to her. I reached into my pocket for the ninepence and I tried my hardest to look poor and helpless.

'How much a week d'ye get for the paper round?'

'Five and tenpence, sir, for two paper rounds, mornin' and evenin'.'

'Bastardin' robbers,' he snorted; 'should be strung up, the lotta them.' He shot a big gollyer out of the window. 'You hang on to the ninepence, I didn't put the flag down anyway.'

'Ah, thanks a million, sir. Yer awful decent,' and I was out of the cab and away down to the shop like a bullet before he got the chance to change his mind.

That evening I sang my head off right to the last paper on the round, and when I got home for tea I couldn't wait to get it over with and be out again. That five shillings was burning a hole in my pocket.

I was on my third slice of bread and jam when Ma came in and I knew at once that she was in some kind of bother. She had a lovely face; stout now, but you could tell that she'd been a real smasher when the oul' fella had first gotten hold of her; but there was a sad expression that she had and it was there in her face so much of the time that it seemed to be built in.

'Ah, hello, Ma. What's up?'

'Ah, nothing, son. Finish yer tea.'

I ate the bread and jam. It wasn't much of a tea for a starving kid like me, but I knew it was the best she could do and I'd have bet money that she hadn't had even one slice for herself. I'd given up trying to get her to eat her share. She had gotten out of the habit of eating and I knew it was a waste of time.

'There's something the matter, Ma. What is it?'

She sank into a chair facing me. She didn't say a word. I took two florrins out of my pocket and she stared at them. It was as if she didn't dare believe her eyes. I put them into her hand.

'Oh, the blessin's a God on you, Paddy.' She looked so relieved, and then the worry came back into her face. 'You didn't lift it, son?'

' 'Course I didn't. What d'you take me for?' I acted all hurt, and God love her she was mortified.

'Ah, sure I knew you didn't, son. I'm sorry,' She smiled a bit. 'I'll tell you one thing, you've saved my life.'

She reached over and touched my hand and I felt marvellous to be able to give her such a lift with a miserable four shillings.

'How's Larry, Ma?'

'Ah, he's a bit better,' She sounded weary. 'Another few days should see a change in him.'

I went into the bedroom, and because I wasn't minding what I was doing I nearly fell over Billy in the tin bath.

'Will you watch where you're bloody well going!' he yelled, covering his thing with the face flannel.

I didn't answer him even if he was two years older than me. I didn't like him and he didn't like me. It was something for which neither of us was responsible, though I suppose the fact that we were so different in every way had a lot to do with it.

He was clean and neat in his habits and he was working very hard to improve himself. I was careless and untidy and I couldn't even think about the next day, let alone the future and all that. So we just lived in the same house and drove each other mad almost every time we came face to face.

But for all the rows and fights that we had I still thought he was a good enough fella, though I'd never have let him know it. I had a grudging respect for him. You just couldn't help it if you knew him. Whatever Billy did, he did well, and had guts to burn. He was afraid of no one, and no matter who he talked with he looked them straight in the eye. He was like a man, really, though he wasn't yet eighteen, but if there was one thing about him that annoyed me it was the way he covered his chopper when you walked in and he was having a bath. You'd think that you were going to swipe it or something.

'I'll never wipe my face with that thing again,' I nodded at the flannel.

'You'll get a belt in the teeth, gabby,' he hissed, his eyes becoming slits in his pink and white face.

I didn't say anything to that. I stepped carefully round the bath to get to Larry in the bed. There were three beds in the room and an old wardrobe, still cracked from the hammer that Ma threw at the oul' fella one day when she was in a temper. There was nothing on the floorboards except dirt, and the wallpaper was the sort of stuff that made kids run away from home.

Larry's head on the pillow was like a big butterfly. His blond, almost white, hair was untidy around his head and his brown eyes were the size of half-dollars. There were dark rings beneath them and he was very pale in the face. He was a feckin' awful nuisance for such a little maggot, but lately I'd started to like him, even though he was the cheekiest little brat on The Hill.

'Gommorrah, Smelly,' I said.

'Ah, shurrup yer mouth.' He shut his eyes at the sight of me.

'Okay, Smelly, if that's the way you want it. I'll keep it for myself.'

His head came up off the pillow and his eyes were wide open.

'Keep what?' He tried a bit too late to sound casual about it.

'None of your business,' I said. 'If you want to be snotty just because you've a bit of the 'flu, I'll give it to one of the other kids.'

'Ah, I'm not well,' he moaned, doing a good copy of my poor mouth. 'I'm sick.'

'You are in my back sick. You can kid Ma with that stuff but you're wasting your time trying it on me.'

I took the apple out of my pocket and held it to him. He grabbed it so quickly that I didn't even get time to tease him a bit. And with one bite he had half of it in his mouth.

'Is that what ye wer' puttin' me under a compliment for?'

I didn't answer him. Slowly I took the *Beano* out of my pocket, watching his eyes go pop when he saw it. There was nothing on God's earth that meant as much to Larry as the *Beano*. I smoothed out the wrinkles and sat there on the edge of the bed. I'd had to scrunch it up when I'd pinched it in the shop, but it wasn't damaged.

I held on to it and I was just about to start making him sweat for it when I realised that he was really miserable. And whether he was acting or not, I just didn't have the heart to tease him. I threw the comic down on the bed and he grabbed it.

'That's three dee you owe me.'

'Ah, I'll pay you when I start work.'

'Work? You work! A little crab like you! The only job you'll ever get will be down in the chemist's shop watching the vanishing cream.'

Larry didn't laugh and at a joke like that you could hardly blame him.

Billy was standing with the towel around him when I turned to get out. He was in my way with his big chest and he didn't look like he was going to move. I made a pretend grab at the towel and he nearly fell backwards into the bath. I ran round him and out the door, with him calling me all the bastards in creation. I nearly had a heart attack from laughing once I was safe out in the kitchen.

Even when Larry got over the 'flu I couldn't help worrying if he was all right. I must have been changing, because up to then I'd never worried about anyone but myself. Now I just couldn't help it. He seemed to be coughing all the time and he was as pale as a glass of milk.

Many times when we were sitting at home I'd see Ma keeping an eye on him, and every time he had a spasm of coughing she went through agony for him. One night, when the oul' fella was there in a bloody awful temper, Larry started to cough. The oul' fella told him to shut up, but Larry couldn't stop. The poor little bastard was tearing his lungs out, it was so bad.

The oul' fella got up to give him a swipe, but before he got near Larry, Ma was on her feet, her eyes wild with anger.

'Lay one finger on that child and I'll swing for you, Maguire.'

There was a chill in her voice that gave me the shivers and the poor oul' fella got the fright of his life. He stood there looking at her for a few seconds and I thought they were going to get stuck into each other. Then he gave a kind of growl in his throat and he went into the bedroom. He slammed the door so hard behind him that I thought it would bring the block down around our ears. It was a week to the day after that that Larry died.

4

GALLOPING consumption, an oul' one up the street said it was. Jeysus help poor little Larry, it must have been galloping. They didn't so much as get time to get him into hospital and he died as he had lived for the past year, coughing his lungs up. And a long while afterwards I found out that Ma had known that he didn't have much time to go, and to think I wondered what she'd been so quiet about all that last week.

She loved us all, I knew that. But Larry was the baby, and even though he was ten or so, he'd never seemed like anything more than a baby. He'd never grown much bigger than a plum and there was always something the matter with him, so that Ma had to give him more attention than any of the rest of us. Poor oul' Ma, was it any wonder she was as grey as a badger?

I hated Larry dying like that, and I wished with all my heart that I'd never hit him that night he'd shit himself with fright in The Prinner. And when I thought about all the times I'd sent him home when he tried to follow me up to The Dodder for a swim I cried until I was dry. It was a bitter lesson and a hard pill to swallow. If you're going to do something for someone do it while they're alive. Prayers and flowers and tears and white-wood satin-lined coffins, and headstones and lines in a newspaper, won't do them much good when they're six feet under.

I felt so helpless too, not being able to do a thing to stop him from dying and not being able to help Ma, except by giving her whatever few shillings I could pick up here there and everywhere.

She never spoke about it, but I knew that she died a little bit the day they lowered Larry into the ground. And two years later she was still paying for the funeral.

There were a lot of people in the church before they took the coffin out to the hearse. Mostly women, Ma's friends. People with more than enough troubles of their own, crying real tears for a little kid they hardly knew. And a few men, sad silent oul' fellas with their caps in their hands paying their last respects. It was a heart-warming thing. With all the kids that were up on The Hill you'd hardly expect anyone to care that one of them might die. Yet they did. They cared and they walked behind a hearse to show that they did. It was all that any of them could do and they did it with a heart and a half.

The oul' fella, my own father, was like a man struck dumb. He didn't say a word to anyone, just nodded his head whenever anyone expressed their sympathy. His face was lined with grey cracks, a mask that hid everything except the desperate helpless thing that was in his eyes. God, but I knew how he felt at that time. The two of us were useless and the more we thought about it the more it bloody well hurt.

I was kneeling down trying to pray for Larry, but I found that I was cursing God for taking him away from us and especially from Ma. She'd had enough pain and misery in her day and Larry had been a light in her life. Was it too much to ask that he be left with her?

This priest then started on about Larry's soul going to a better place and all the rest of it. Phrases like greener pastures and God's holy will and more and more of the same until I thought I'd puke all over the seat. Then Ma began to wail. It burst out of her and it was heartbreaking to listen to, and I bit into my hand until the blood came to my lips, and under my breath I swore and effed and blinded God from a height, and then I ran blindly out of the church and I swore on my life that I'd never go back into one again, as long as I lived.

I thought my lungs would burst, but I didn't stop running until I reached the banks of The Dodder and I was so worn out that I crumpled into the grass near the water. I lay on my face and I cried, draining myself of the soreness and the pain and the endless, ever-present helpless feeling that was so much a part of me. And when the tears stopped it was because there wasn't anything left in me.

After a long time I stood up and shakily walked the narrow path that led to Orwell Bridge. This place, this neglected river and its banks, was one long happy memory to me. I'd learned to swim in this water, holding on to an old petrol tin and kicking my feet, then working my way into the dog's paddle and later the breast stroke. And I'd seen my heroes dive off the bridge into the dangerous, dirty, shallow water for a bet of sixpence, and I'd seen Plunkett get caught in the weeds and myself and half a dozen other kids pull him out. We adored Plunkett because he was the best swimmer we'd ever seen.

Now this place was just ground under my feet, something to walk on and not to think about. A place to be alone in and in which to feel sorry for yourself. An empty place that was empty because that was how I felt inside.

So there I was, busy feeling sorry for myself, walking along the river bank, not even thinking of the state my face must have been in after all the tears. Three fellas, they must have been mitching from school, I suppose, came along and when they saw my face they started name calling and jeering me for being a cry baby. I went wild with anger. Never in my life before had I wanted so much to be left alone. I must have gone wild to fight three of them, because normally I would have weighed up the odds and somehow talked my way out of it.

I knocked one of them, a freckle-faced bastard with flat eyes, into the middle of the river and for all I cared he could have drowned on the spot. But the other two got stuck into me and though I lashed out left, right and centre, they really did beat the bejeysus out of me before they ran off and left me lying in my own blood and vomit.

My face was bruised and my mouth was bleeding badly, but I just didn't care about that. I thumped the ground in exasperation, wanting to kill the three bastards who'd done this to me and even more so for bothering me when I wanted so badly to be on my own. Then I vomited again and lay in it for a long time.

When I did get up I walked to Mrs. Kearney's in Terenure, and when she opened the door I was so pleased to see her that I'm sure I would have cried if I hadn't been dry as a bone.

She gave me whiskey to drink. It was so hot that it hurt my throat and chest and then it was warm like a coal inside, and I told her everything. She was ever so kind to me, holding me like a baby until I fell asleep on the couch. By the time I drifted off I'd even forgotten how much I hated to have anyone feel sorry for me except myself.

It was well into the evening when I woke up and I was still sore, inside and out. I drank strong coffee with whiskey in it, and after that had put life back into me she put me into a hot bath with lashings of disinfectant in the water for my cuts and bruises. And that night I slept with her, holding on to her all the time, and if I snuggled into her breasts it was only to get comfort that I knew Ma couldn't give me.

In the morning I remembered that I hadn't done the paper round the previous evening, and I thought shag the paper round and the oul' one in the shop and shag everybody else too except Ma and Mrs. Kearney. God, I still felt awful bad about Larry.

I ate a really big breakfast and only when I'd cleaned the plate did I realise how hungry I'd been. Mrs. Kearney talked to me about Larry and she was kind and full of understanding and you could tell that she was very fond of me from the way she spoke. And when she finished I felt a little bit better. There was nothing I could do for Larry, not while he was alive or after he was dead. It was the way things were and very likely the way things would always be for me. But about one thing I was sure, whether he'd been a cheeky little gett or not, I was awful glad to have had him for my brother.

Later in the morning I had another bath and Mrs. Kearney washed me all over with pink soap. Then we got back into bed and I told her that I loved her and I meant it when I said it. And she loved me, she said, and she'd come to need me, and there in the bed, thinking about it, I didn't mind at all. She'd been a real pal to me when I needed her help, and I wouldn't forget that, not ever.

It was only when I got out of bed that I thought about Ma. God only knew what agony I'd caused her by staying out all night. I got my clothes on as quickly as I could. Suddenly I couldn't wait to get home to make sure that Ma was all right.

Mrs. Kearney gave me a parcel, and when I opened it I found a new pair of grey flannel trousers. I put them on, sticking my own pair into the paper, and then I kissed her goodbye, at the same time thanking her for being so good to me. On the way home I rubbed a few bits of clay into the legs, just to take the very new look off them.

Ma didn't fight with me when I got in. She was only too relieved to see me and I told her a cock-and-bull story about walking all night, and we cried a bit together and I think she understood how big a blow Larry's death had been to me. The oul' fella tried to give me a ballocking, but she told him to shut up and leave me alone. She seemed old for the first time in her life. Even the grey hair hadn't made her seem old before, and I thought it was a stinking shame that Ma should have that happen to her.

I told her that I'd found the flannels and I tried to tell her in a way that might have made her think I'd pinched them. She wouldn't like that, but in her present state I didn't think she'd be too worried. I was well pleased with them. They were near enough the right fit, and that evening when I went down to the paper shop I felt all grown up in my first pair of longers.

The oul' one in the shop must have heard about Larry being dead because she didn't say one word to me about not turning up the night before. In all the time I'd worked for her she hadn't spoken a dozen words to me and to this day I'm not sure what her name was. I didn't say anything to her either. I just couldn't have cared less about her or her paper round, even though I did need the money to help Ma.

In the course of the next few days I really felt the impact of owning a pair of long trousers. It took a bit of getting used to, but every time I touched the material I got a great kick out of it. And because most of the other kids were green with envy I felt even better.

It was about a week after Larry died that the oul' fella and the two eldest brothers went off to Manchester. Just like that, as if they were going up to Milltown to watch Shamrock Rovers play Bohemians. There were no tears, just quick, short, vacant goodbyes, and Ma was left with me and Billy and the sister, Josie.

Up until then, I'd hardly ever given the oul' fella a second thought, I didn't like him and he acted as though I was an eyesore, so we kept away from each other as much as we could. But when he'd left the house I found myself wondering what would happen to him. Would he be all right? Would he miss me and Ma and the others? And would he ever find happiness, any sort of happiness, to lift the grey clouds out of his eyes?

I didn't know him well. He was one man who never wasted a word in his life, and whatever stories I'd heard about him hadn't come to me from his lips. I'd heard often enough from Ma about him fighting 'The Tans' and 1916 and the times that followed. Stories of shootings and explosions and scampering retreats across roof-tops. Of a night when the oul' fella was taking her to the pictures at The De Luxe, in Aungiers Street.

She had taken his revolver and put it down the front of her dress. The Tans had appeared and they beat him up while they searched him for firearms. And one of them, pretending to search her, had felt her breasts, not knowing that the gun was between them and that she was thanking God that she had taken it from the oul' fella. She knew that he would have shot them down before they'd had time to lay a finger on him and that he would have gone on to enjoy the picture all the more for having done it.

You could say he was a hard man, the product of a rough school. I'd seen him myself, fighting a man who was half his size again, and as it started I remember being terrified for him. Maybe not so much for him as for myself. On The Hill, if your Da got licked in a fight, it meant that you had to stand endless jeering and jibing or be always fighting yourself.

I didn't like fighting and if I was terrified that day it was because I thought the oul' fella was really in for it. I was wrong. He punched and kicked and used his head like a man gone mad, and even when the other oul' fella fell down, out to the world, the Da was still putting the boot in. A few of the neighbours had to drag him off and it was a few minutes before he got a grip of himself. Then he was like a fella who had just got out of bed, he didn't seem to remember being in a fight at all and I never heard him mention it again. I suppose I was sort of grateful to him that day.

Now he was gone to Manchester and I felt that I knew why he was so bitter and so unhappy. He had done his bit when he was needed, risking his very life for a belief in an ideal. He fought with a lot of others like him for his own country, risking his neck for the right to live and breathe like an Irishman. And when it was all over he and the others tramped the streets looking for employment with little hope of finding it. So he'd had to sit and watch his children go hungry and barefooted and him helpless to do anything about it. And, finally, the death of his youngest son and the trip to Manchester, England. The just reward of a grateful nation. I loved him that day and I was truly proud of him.

Andy and Tommy, the eldest brothers, went with him, but that didn't mean a thing to me, any more than Larry's death had affected them. I suppose they were good enough fellas, I don't know, but I would willingly have swopped the pair of them for little Larry.

Things changed in the house after that and it was much better all round. For a start there was more room. I even had a bed to myself, and apart from Josie there wasn't anyone to push me around. She didn't like me at all and I really and truly hated the sight of her. She was always dolling herself up, which she didn't need to do, because she was nice enough looking with her red hair and her green eyes. I suppose it was because she was twenty years old that she thought she was entitled to boss Billy and me.

Well, if she didn't get far with me, with Billy she got nowhere. You had to give it to him; he stood up to her, and no matter how much she shouted and threatened, he paid not one scrap of attention to her.

When she had a go at me I kept my mouth shut because she'd give you a box in the lug as quick as look at you. But when her back was turned I used to call her all the bitches under the sun and I convinced myself that she was as ugly as a pig and that she had the biggest arse in the city of Dublin.

It was good for Ma to have her there, though, and for this reason I could stand the sight of her. I suppose Ma could talk to her in a way that she never could to Billy and me. And, Jeysus, could that Josie talk! Honest to God, you never heard anything like it in your whole life. She was a telephone operator in a sausage company, so I suppose it was an advantage, but she kept on so much that it was enough to give you cauliflower ears. But she was good to Ma in her own way, and if only she hadn't been so bossy and so bloody gabby I think I might have gotten to like her.

Billy was getting on well at work now and he was very proud of the fact that one day he was going to be a heating engineer. He'd started off as teaboy and general dogsbody and he was now officially an apprentice to the trade. He loved the work and he got on well with his employers and the other fellas on the job and he seemed to be completely happy. He was a hard worker and even then you could tell he'd do well in life. The sort of fella that could do anything once he put his mind to it, and if he wanted something, he saved every penny he got until he had enough. And he never asked anybody for anything in his whole life and that's not a bad thing in a fella.

So far I still didn't have a steady job, but I didn't worry about it. I still made more money than most fellas of my age and I didn't have to take orders from anyone. Ma didn't bother me about it. I think she felt that I'd get a job when I was good and ready.

Some days I wouldn't earn anything, but it didn't matter all that much. I could always nick something. This wasn't difficult for me. I seemed to have some kind of gift for getting my hands on things, so that one way or another I was always coming into a few bob.

Anyway, with my education, or the lack of it, I didn't think I'd find it too easy to get a job that was worth while. I had a Primary Certificate from the National School, but then a well-trained mongrel could have passed that examination if you gave him a condition powder first.

You had to get eighty out of two hundred in English, Irish and arithmetic. I was all right at the English. I loved writing compositions and the printed page was kind to my eyes. I had to struggle through the arithmetic, making sure that I kept the paper as neat as a raindrop, but the Irish was the biggest sweat of my life. I just couldn't grasp Irish. It was as if I had a mental block where it was concerned. I suppose I felt that it was a waste of time. Most of the fellas in the school were going to end up in England, anyway.

When the marks were announced I found that I'd got a hundred and forty in English, one hundred and ten in arithmetic and eighty-three in Irish. Well, I got a pass, but as you can judge I was no genius. So what kind of job could I hope to get? I was over the fifteen mark and I could talk with the best, but when it came to producing pass certificates with your name on them I was way down the line. Still, the very fact that I was wondering about work meant I was getting ready to start. And I wasn't getting any younger. Also, I wanted a bicycle of my own. To get one I would have to have a steady wage coming in. Promises and good intentions weren't any good to the hire-purchase companies. And who could blame them.

It was Harry Redmond who gave me the push I needed and it happened in the same way that he'd told me about women. You had to give it to that Redmond. For a fella who never got any further than the banks of the Dodder, he was awful well educated. Every day in the library he read all the papers and he seemed to remember every single line. And that's the truth. It was as if he had the very paper there inside his head. Anyway, it was Harry suggested that I go into the insurance business.

I burst out laughing when he said it and I think he would have got up and walked away, only I'd promised to buy him a bottle of stout if he got me into the pub with him.

'Ah, for Jeysus' sake, Harry, what do I know about insurance?'

He gave me a look and you could tell he felt awful superior. I had to wait for my answer too, while he made a slow job of taking a cough sweet out of a tin and sticking it in his mouth. Then he took out a butt and lit that up and took a drag on it before he said a word.

'What would anyone who was thinking of giving you a job expect you to know at seventeen?'

'Seventeen,' I said, 'what're y'on about? I'm not even sixteen yet.'

'There you go.' He sounded weary. 'How in the name of Christ do you expect to get anywhere in this world if you haven't got imagination?' He took another drag at the butt. 'Nobody's going to give you anything if you tell them the truth. Do you think I'd have done all those mots if I'd told them the truth? 'Course I wouldn't. I tell them I'm a poet or a writer or a painter, depending on the mood I'm in. I recite them a few lines of Shakespeare or Yeats, and then I tell them I wrote it. That's what I do.'

I didn't know much about the men he'd just mentioned but it seemed obvious that they were writers of some sort.

'But don't they know you didn't write it?'

'Know?' He smiled with his crooked mouth. 'The dames that frequent the banks of the Dodder couldn't read a bleedin' paper, let alone know anything about poetry. Anyway, if you go and tell the insurance people that you're seventeen they don't expect you to take over the running of an office, now do they?'

When you thought about it that seemed fairly sensible. I couldn't help smiling. There was more in Redmond's head than a fine comb would take out.

'They take you in expecting to teach you the game. That's why you go in so young.'

'I was thinking more of the building game, carpentry or something.'

His lips swelled up with the sneer he gave me. 'Carpentry or something. Will you stop, for Jeysus' sake. Any ballocks can be a carpenter or a bricklayer, it's easy if you've got two hands and a pair of eyes, but once you start, that's all you'll ever be. There's no way out of that game except in a box. Anyway, ten or fifteen years from now, machines'll be doing the carpentry and they'll be shoving buildings up in one piece. I'm telling you, tradesmen are on the way out. You take it from me, boy, you don't want to get into that lark. Get into insurance for a start.

No matter how they build places they have to be insured. And the way things'll be going in a few years you won't be able to get a car on the roads. There won't be enough room for them all and they've all got to be insured. In the end, just about everything has to be covered by insurance.'

'Anyway,' he said, 'who are you going to meet if you work in the building line? A load of bogmen that don't know any better, and after a few years of it you'll be as thick as they are. Now, in insurance you've got chances of meeting people who might be able to do you some good. Nice mots that live in decent places, blokes in good positions who might take a fancy to you and help you get a better job. If you want to make something of yourself you've got to get a good start.'

He stood up and I knew he wanted that Guinness I'd promised him. We walked over to Campion's and he took a quick look in the snug.

'Come on,' he said. 'You're all right.'

I followed him in and he ordered a bottle of Guinness for himself and a Bulmer's cider for me. I slipped him two shillings, and while he paid the barman I took a look around at the dark panelled room with its soft-topped seats and the tiny hole in the wall where you went for service.

He came back to the table and only I held out my hand, the change would have gone straight into his pocket. He sat down and he gave the stout an awful quick death. Then he sat there licking the froth from his lips as I sipped at the cider. I liked it, the taste was sweet and it didn't seem all that strong. After I'd finished it I paid for another round and Harry kept on about the insurance game. He gave me such a line that after two ciders I felt as though I could have run The Insurance Corporation of Ireland.

'I'm seventeen, sir,' I said to the man in the insurance brokers. 'I see.' He wrote it down after my name and address and he looked at me from behind his dark-rimmed glasses. 'Why do you feel you'd like to work in insurance, Mr. Maguire?'

'I'm thinking of the future, sir.' I said. 'I believe that in ten or fifteen years buildings will be going up so fast and there will be so many cars on the roads that there'll be some wonderful chances in insurance.'

'Really?' He looked a bit surprised.

'Oh, yes, sir.' I nodded my head earnestly. 'In ten years or so I don't think the roads will be able to cope with all the cars that will be on them and with improved building techniques premises will be going up faster all the time.'

I was hoping that I'd said it just right, the way Redmond had told me to. He'd coached me on it for the best part of an hour and when he'd said it it had sounded marvellous. The man in the glasses looked at me hard and I sat through it like a well-washed angel. I thought I looked all right. Harry's suit was a bit baggy, but it was clean and I'd had a good scrub and combed my hair.

'Have you been to a Christian Brothers School, Mr. Maguire?'

I'd known that this would come and if it hadn't been for Redmond's coaching I'd have been lost.

'I couldn't go to one, sir.'

'And why was that?'

'Well, sir, things weren't too good at home. My mother just couldn't afford to send me. I had to do paper rounds and anything else that I could to help her run the house, sir. And since she lost my little brother I had to more or less look after her, sir.'

He didn't say anything for a minute and I held on to my breath.

'Have you got your birth certificate, Mr. Maguire?'

Redmond had even prepared me for this and I only hoped I had the guts to put it over.

'I went for it when I was coming for the interview, sir. I nearly didn't come to see you.'

'Why was that, Mr. Maguire?'

'Well, sir, it's not an easy thing to admit. I found out that my mother and father weren't actually married when I was born. It was an awful shock, sir.'

He was stunned for a second and I almost felt sorry for the poor bastard, but I could just see Redmond sitting on the seat by the corner of Leinster Road and him just knowing that his formula was going to work. The man took off his glasses and he rubbed the thumb and forefinger of his right hand into the corners of his eyes.

'You're a very courageous young man, Mr. Maguire. We would be prepared to pay you thirty shillings a week for a trial period of one month.'

'Oh, that'd be great, sir. Thank you very much.'

'If you prove satisfactory, as I'm sure you will, we would give you a small increase and you would receive an annual increment from then on.'

'Thank you, sir,' I said, and meant it. 'I won't let you down.'

'I'm sure you won't, Mr. Maguire.' He smiled at me and I liked him.

He told me that I would receive a letter confirming my appointment. Then he stood up and shook my hand, and as I left the office I realised why I liked him so much—he kept on calling me Mr. Maguire.

The letter came next morning. I was to start work as office boy, though they called it junior clerk, and I would be paid the sum of thirty shillings per week for a trial period of one month. All the things he'd told me, typed on nice white paper with engraving, and it was signed by the man I'd spoken to at the office. His name was S. L. Hayes and I thought how good he had been to me. He was a really kind man and he proved one thing to me, that with a little effort people can be nice to each other.

But thinking how nice he was made me feel a bit guilty at

46

having told him all those lies. And, Jeysus, if Ma ever found out that I'd told him that lie about her not being married when I was born she'd throw a blue fit. But what else could I do? I wouldn't have gotten the job if I'd told the truth and if he'd seen my birth certificate. He'd have known I wasn't even sixteen and the advert had said that the applicant must be seventeen.

As I say, he was a nice man and I felt awful at having to tell him the tale. But at a time like that, when so much depends on it, a fella has to do the best he can and worry about it afterwards. Not that I worried all that much.

5

Ma was used to my independent nature, but even she was surprised when I showed her the letter. She was pleased. You could see that in her eyes and in the proud way she held the letter even after she'd finished reading it. Then she looked worried. What was I going to wear to the office? she asked me. That was a right shock, because, ridiculous as it might seem, I hadn't given it a thought.

Stupid but true. I hadn't even considered the fact that I had no clothes to wear. I'd gone to the interview in Redmond's suit and afterwards I'd given it back to him. Maybe not ever having a suit of my own had something to do with it. If you've never had a suit it's not easy to include a suit in your thinking. Unless you happen to be a fella who thinks of little else but clothes, and at that time nothing could have been further from my mind.

That evening Ma was still fretting because she couldn't see any way of getting me some clobber. I was thinking of a gas meter or even two or three. Some of the meters in the neighbourhood weren't worth knocking off, but if I were to go up along Palmerston Road I might find a shilling one that was full up. I wasn't in the least bit bothered about doing the job, but I didn't want to get into any trouble, not now, when I was about to start my first real bit of employment. I was still in a puzzle when, like the answer to a prayer, the oul' fella in Manchester came through.

There were six English pound notes in the envelope and a slip of paper with his address written on it. He hadn't written a letter or even a note, he wasn't that kind of man. But it didn't matter. He must have cared about us to let us know where he was, and the money showed that he wanted to help us.

Poor Ma, she had to sit down and count the money again and again before she could believe that she wasn't imagining things. That was one of the awful sad things, that state people get into when they don't even expect any relief to their endless predicament.

She kept looking too at the paper with the address on it, and then quietly, rocking her grey head backwards and forwards, she began to cry. I didn't say anything. I just stood there with my hand on her shoulder. God knows, she was entitled to cry if ever a woman was. Without feeling the least bit sorry for herself, she was entitled to cry for all the things that might have been.

I suppose she must have loved the oul' fella at some time in her life and I honestly think that if he'd come through the door at that moment he'd have got a kiss and a hug and a hundred thousand welcomes. As I stood there beside Ma I swore to myself that no matter how long it took me I'd pay him back for sending that six quid when it was so badly needed, and I tried to ignore the guilt that I felt for all the times I'd called him an oul' bastard behind his back.

The suit was tweed and it was the colour of the heather above at Glencree on the Dublin Mountains. It didn't have much of a cut to it but it was the best suit I'd ever seen. Ma paid two pounds five for it and you could see the happiness in her, just to be able to give. I got a new pair of shoes as well. Brown brogues, they were, and a shirt and tie to go with the suit.

Billy went black with jealousy when he saw me all dressed up and I nearly drove him mad from looking at myself in the big mirror on the sideboard. So much so that he gave me a punch in the thigh that really hurt me, but I let on I wasn't

49

bothered about it and kept on admiring myself. Ma told me off for being so vicious and she explained to Billy that I had to have the suit to start work on Monday. You could see he understood that, but he still hated me for having it, and I suppose that I'd have felt the same if it had been the other way round, except I'd have hated him twice as much.

About nine o'clock that Saturday evening I walked up through Gulistan Terrace and the cottages, and on up into the laneway that led to Rathmines, and I felt like a film star. My skin was tingling with excitement and I had springs on my heels and I was as tall as the town hall clock. I was only sorry it was fairly dark because it cut down my chances of being seen in the new gear.

When I got as far as The Stella I stood around for a good ten minutes hoping that someone I knew would see me. I wanted to be told how good I looked and I thought that I might even get off with a bird. No such luck, it just got bloody chilly standing there. I was shivering by the time I decided to go and have a drink.

Outside Campion's I came to a full stop. I just couldn't seem to find the courage to go in. I felt that everyone would be looking at me the minute I stepped inside. And only a few minutes before I'd been standing outside The Stella, hoping that people would notice me. Talk about being mixed up.

Just then one of the regulars came along and as he went in I took a deep breath and followed on his heels. Redmond was there and I was more than glad to see him. He looked up, but I don't think it registered that it was me standing there. Then his eyes popped a bit and his twisted mouth went even more crooked in disbelief. I knew then that I looked all right. Harry Redmond wasn't easily impressed.

I gave him a wink with the left eye and I went to the hole in the wall and ordered two pints of Guinness in my best movie voice. The barman didn't give me a second look, which was okay from the point of view of me getting served with the gargle and me being under age, but I was a bit let down that he didn't throw another glance at the suit.

When I carried the drinks over to the table Redmond still looked a bit surprised. He looked at the tall glasses and you could see that me being on pints as well didn't help him at all. But, as you might expect, he soon adopted his 'couldn't care less' face, and when he didn't even remark on the suit I could willingly have poured the pint, my very first pint of Guinness, all over him.

'Pints now, is it, Maguire?'

'Yeh,' I said. 'I got you one as well.'

'I should feckin' well think so, and me sitting here nursing a dead glass.'

He lifted the tumbler and swallowed half the pint. He put it down again and when I lifted mine he was watching me with both eyes. It wasn't easy to look casual. Drinking your first pint with a past master like Redmond looking at you took a bit of doing. I took a big mouthful and it went down all right.

'Not bad,' I said.

'It's an acquired taste,' he said, pulling out another of his filthy butts and lighting it. 'A few weeks on that stuff and you'll never want to drink anything else as long as you live.'

Right there and then I didn't agree with him, but as it turned out he wasn't far wrong. Honestly, that Redmond knew so much about everything that he could have gone places if he hadn't been such a shagging layabout. He could even have made a living showing people how easy it was to put away twenty or thirty pints of stout.

By Monday morning, Saturday's drinking was just about out of my head and I was out bright and early with the paper rounds. It was a fine morning for early March. Not cold and mean like it often was, just bright and clear like the start of a good day. I was glad it was nice. It was as if it would be a good day to start work and I wondered what it would be like to be employed in an insurance office.

I couldn't remember what the office was like. I'd been so excited before the interview, so busy trying to remember all that Redmond had pumped into me, that I didn't take it in. Not that it mattered, it was just that it was a thrill to even think of going there. And it wasn't only the thirty bob a week. It was being old enough to start a decent job, and the new suit, and a sort of looking forward to doing something new, something, as Harry Redmond said, that could lead to better things and a life away from The Hill.

Even when I got home for my breakfast I felt it was a big day in my life. And I was glad to be doing all this thinking about it because then it wouldn't pass by like any other day. Not that it was my first big day. When I'd gotten that boxcart with the one and sixpenny shafts; when Mrs. Kearney had given me my first pair of long trousers; they were big days. And the day I'd had the cake all to myself. I think that was the biggest of them all up to going to work in the office.

It was rare for any of us in the family to get more than one slice of cake at a time. There were so many of us at home that there was only ever one slice each. Ma used to share it out as best she could and I can't remember seeing her have so much as half a slice herself. So it became a big thing with me. I used to spend ages looking in at the cakes in the window of The Monument Creamery, dreaming of getting one all to myself.

When I got the box of flags to sell I had no intention of keeping any of the money like the other kids were doing. Even when I saw some of them juggling with a knife in the slit on top of the box. I didn't think it was right. And I didn't do it because it seemed like a lousy thing to do. Until one day in Rathmines as I passed the shop. I knew that if I didn't have a whole cake to myself just once, I'd go mad for thinking about it.

I ran all the way home, pushing the guilty feeling into the

back of my mind. I took the box from where I'd hidden it under the bed and I climbed out through the back window into the drying yards behind our flat. I put the box down on the grass and smashed it to pieces with a brick that I'd found nearby.

As fast as I could I picked up the coins and put them in my pocket, then I picked up the bits of wood and on the way down to the bus stop on Ranelagh Road scattered them about the streets.

Twenty-seven shillings. I counted it again and again on the way into O'Connell Street on the bus. It was a lot of dough and I was too excited at having such an amount to be even frightened at what I'd just done.

Near the Carlton Cinema there was a big cake shop, and when I looked into the window I saw a beauty of a cake that made me weak just to look at it. I went in and asked to buy it and the oul' one behind the counter gave me a funny look. Not that you could blame her. I was still in short trousers and I couldn't have been much to look at.

She put it into a box and took my five and sixpence and when I walked out of the shop it felt like a ton weight in my hand. I paid for a one and eightpenny seat and went up to the balcony in the Carlton and I sat there in the dark and ate every single crumb. It was a great feeling and I felt so good that I didn't begin to look at the film until I'd thrown the empty box on the floor.

I sat back then to enjoy the picture. It was called *Step Lively* and Frank Sinatra and George Murphy and Gloria de Haven were in it. It was a musical and I loved all the songs and the dancing and I thought that George Murphy had the most Irish face that I'd ever seen on a man. Well, that was a big day, but at the time I didn't think about it, so it just passed by like all the others. But starting work. That was different.

Ma was excited too. Hopping about the kitchen like a hen on a hot plate and after I'd had my porridge she gave me an egg to myself. I can tell you I felt very important that morning.

By ten minutes to nine I was standing outside the office door, and even though I was nervous I couldn't wait to get inside and start my job. Just before nine a fella of about eighteen came along and opened up. I told him who I was and that I was to start work and he shook my hand and made me welcome and he told me that his name was Jack Sloane.

We went into the office and he opened the inside of the post box and took out the letters. Then, using the counter as a desk, he began to open the post and he told me that he had just been promoted, which was why the firm needed a new office boy. Without being a mind-reader you could tell that he was pleased with himself, but he was nice with it and I liked him.

He was only my height, but he was well built with it, and from the way he spoke you could tell he'd been to a Christian Brothers school. Even Dublin blokes that went to those schools ended up with a touch of brogue in their voices. It must have been due to the fact that most of the Brothers came from the country and not from the city itself.

By the time Jack had sorted out the letters other people were beginning to arrive. There were several girls who weren't too bad to look at and Jack blushed when he said good morning to them. I was kind of sorry for him, being shy like, but in another way I was glad. It made up a bit for the difference in our ages and I didn't feel so much of a kid.

He showed me a table with a single long drawer in it and he said that this would be my desk. There was a hard-backed foolscap-sized book, into which I was to enter the name from every letter before it was posted. That was all right by me. I loved writing and I had a new six-bob pen in my pocket that I was just dying to use. There was also a bundle of economy labels that I was to use on old envelopes for the morning hand delivery.

That first morning Jack came with me and he showed me all the offices within reasonable walking distance of our own to which I would deliver letters. He seemed to enjoy the walk, saying that it made a break from the office. I didn't say anything. I was thinking that I did enough shagging walking with the papers while he was still in bed. Also, I thought that he probably felt that way because he didn't have to do it any more.

The third office on the route was a filthy place, a small firm of brokers with all kinds of girls running about everywhere. You could tell that Jack thought it was the greatest place in town, and when one or two of the mots had a bit of crack with him he blushed again. There was one girl there that I thought was a real smasher, and once again it was the tight sweater across big breasts that got me going.

She was blonde and very pretty and she had a pair of wicked blue eyes, but it was her yellow sweater and what was inside it that made the biggest impression on me. Jack told me that her name was Maureen Murphy, and all through the rest of the delivery I couldn't stop myself from dreaming about her breasts and what it would be like to get my hand on them.

Back in our office I had a quick look around. There were six typists and a switchboard operator. She caught my eye first because she looked so fast and common, but when she talked on the phone she put on a voice and it was a scream to listen to her. Later on I used to hear her talking to fellas on the phone and the office manager, a pale-faced snot called Cahill, was always on at her to cut it out. She used to smile at him as though she was putting him on a promise and he never made much of a scene about it. I liked her for that. She had sex appeal to burn and she knew it and she used it when it was likely to be a help to her.

That first morning Cahill didn't say a word to me. I was a bit surprised, because Jack had warned me to expect something. He said that Cahill liked to get stuck into people from the off, hoping that after that they would be ready to run whenever he called.

About three in the afternoon someone stopped by my table

and when I looked up it was Cahill. I got to my feet. Harry Redmond had pumped it into me about being at a psychological disadvantage when you had a fella looking down at you. I was as tall as he was, although he must have been forty years of age.

'Can you write, Maguire?' he sneered at me with a mouth like a bowl of dripping.

Jack had told me that Cahill was married and just then I wondered to myself how any woman could stand the sight of that sneer every day of her life. Jeysus help you, ma'am! I thought.

'Yes, sir, I can,' I said.

'Good, good.' He was grinning now, showing me his off-white teeth. 'I want you to make copies of those.'

He handed me two long forms. They were motor insurance proposal forms, but *he* didn't tell me that, Jack Sloane did. Then he walked back to his desk without another word. I knew then that Jack had done me a favour by warning me. I was hurt, but not as badly as I'd have been if Cahill and his arrogant attitude had been totally unexpected.

Coming down that morning I'd thought that everything would be great in the office. I'd felt so good, like a bird bursting to sing in the spring morning, but as I took the proposal forms up to Jack's desk to ask his advice I realised that there would always be a Cahill about, and, more often than not, more than one.

Jack Sloane had a gift for explaining things. I listened carefully to what he said and he never had to tell me anything more than once. He was a good fella, and when I'd finished the copying of the forms I showed them to him and he okayed them before I took them back to Cahill. Then Jack showed me how to use the franking machine and I thought that was the greatest thing ever. You didn't have to lick one single stamp.

The post began to get signed and I was on my own, folding the letters and double-checking to make sure that the right one went into the right envelope. Stamping them with the franking machine and entering them into the post book. Responsibility. Only the post, I know, but it was great to be completely in charge of something.

Jack had warned me to keep the post trays clear and this meant doing a sort of a round. Cahill's tray first, then into Mr. Hayes' office and finally into Mr. D. J. Henley, the managing director. Mr. Henley was a fine man, big and happy, and I took to him straight away. He never made me feel that I was just an office boy, and in all the time I worked in his firm, he never said a cross word to me.

During that first post I was expecting Mr. Hayes to speak to me every time I went into his office to get the letters, but he was so busy that he never even looked up. Even that first day I could see that he held the firm together. He was cool in his every movement and he made decisions with the ease of a man who was born to be a boss. And yet, somehow he was all right with it, as though he took time to be nice even if he didn't feel like it.

The staff knocked off at five o'clock and in my innocence I thought that meant me too. Fine, I thought, I'd have plenty of time to get up to do the paper round without having to kill myself rushing. The oul' one in the shop didn't like me to be late. God, was I kidding myself? For some reason Cahill didn't seem to be in a rush to get home. In the middle of signing the last batch of letters he rung up one of his pals and had a great bit of crack with him, and me standing there like a feckin' eejit waiting for the post. Finally I got away but by the time I reached the paper shop it was twenty past six.

The oul' cow never even gave me a chance to explain what had happened. She attacked me with her ugly mouth the minute I stepped inside the door. Well, with the humour I was in after getting messed about by Cahill it was too much. I needed that little paper job, but I just couldn't swallow all the things that oul' one said, so I told her to get stuffed and to shove the shop and the newspapers right up her arse, and I walked out without even asking her to pay me for the morning delivery. She ran to the door after me, threatening to tell the Parish Priest that I'd sworn at her, but I didn't even look back at her bacon face. If there was one man in Rathmines that I couldn't have cared less about it was the P.P., or, as he was known to the kids, Little Jesus himself.

When I got home I told Ma about the barney in the shop. She told me not to worry, that it didn't matter. The job in the office had to come first, she said, there was no point in trying to cut myself in halves for an extra few bob a week. So I began one job in the morning and finished another in the same evening. One way or another, it had turned out to be a busy Monday.

After tea I went up on the bus to see Mrs. Kearney. I was over the annoyance that the oul' one had brought out of me. I was glad about that. It was good to be able to bounce right back after a row or a fight. It meant that you'd stopped thinking about it and your mind was free for other things.

Mrs. Kearney was delighted to hear that I'd gotten on so well in the office, and from the way she went on you'd have thought that within about eighteen months I'd have been running the place. Still, whether she talked rubbish or not, she was a great woman for giving you a lift when you were down, and when I told her about losing the paper job she gave me five bob on the spot and said she could afford to give me that much each week. That was a real break, because the job in the butcher's was out too, now that I had to work in the office on Saturday mornings.

I told her how grateful I was, acting my head off as I said it, and by the time I finished I nearly had myself in tears, let alone her. But I meant what I said. She was good to me, and a few minutes later when she leaned over to be kissed and she ran her hand across the flat of my stomach, I knew she was dying for it. That was one of the things I liked best about her, when she wanted it she never made any bones about it. As a matter of fact, if you didn't give it to her she was quite prepared to help herself.

She was full and generous in her every action and she taught me that there was more to love-making than just pushing and pulling. She made me take my time, teaching me to resist the urge to rush like a bull at a gate. She put a lot of effort into me, Mrs. Kearney did, and yet all the time I was lying there with her that night I was thinking of a little blonde with blue eyes and a tight yellow sweater, and her name was Maureen.

6

O N THE Tuesday morning I didn't get up until eight o'clock, and for me that was a real luxury. All that chat about rising in the early morning being a pleasure is a load of old rubbish. Most of the people who say it don't have to get up till noon, anyway.

Going down to town in the bus, I thought about how much things had changed for me in the past week, and there was no denying it was all on account of Harry Redmond.

He'd talked me into going for the interview and he'd coached me on what to say, even down to the bastard bit about the birth certificate. So getting the job was more his doing than mine. Then I'd lost the paper rounds, and the butcher's job was gone on account of Saturday mornings in the office. Now there was a new income of a dollar a week from Mrs. Kearney and I'd had a good sleep-in for the first time in years. And I had a new suit and shoes and shirt, so was it any wonder that as the bus pushed down through Aungiers Street, and on down towards the city itself, life felt good to me? It would have been perfect altogether if only I didn't have to go back to The Hill.

Dreams and more dreams until I got off the bus. All the way down I just sat there dreaming, wishing that this would happen and that would happen, and that everything would be a step away from the flats, and the dirty hungry little kids, and the open dustbin in the hallway and the women up the pole all the time, and the endless rows and fights that went on all around me every time I went back to The Hill. And by the time I got to the office I was fed-up. It was as bad as that. I couldn't even sit and dream without The Hill bringing me back down to earth and back to the flats.

I was preparing the hand-delivery envelopes when this fella I hadn't seen before came up and introduced himself. His name was Larry Deegan and he was a trainee inspector. He'd been out with a client all day Monday, which was why I hadn't seen him. He was like a slim version of Victor Mature, about twenty-six, and we were friends from that first handshake.

He was very different to Jack Sloane. Jack was one of the best, but there was something slick about Larry that appealed to me. And when I saw later on how he handled Cahill he was a hero in my eyes. He wore a suit that had been made to measure and he smoked American fags.

At least three of the mots in the place were after him and he knew it. He used to give them plenty of chat, but I don't think he ever bothered with any of them. The one on the switchboard used to pull her stockings up all the way when he was talking to her, and he used to grin at her and say:

'Nice pair of pins you got there, kid,' and she used to be double-choked at the way he said 'kid'.

Mr. Hayes called me in that morning and he shook my hand and asked me to sit down. I was really grateful to that man. He just had a way of making you feel that you mattered a bit.

'Well, Mr. Maguire, are you going to be happy with us?'

'Oh, yes, sir, I love the work and everybody's been very kind.'

'Good,' he smiled, and opened a packet of cigarettes. 'Would you like to smoke, Mr. Maguire?'

'No, thank you very much all the same, sir.' Redmond had told me to always refuse fags from a superior.

Mr. Hayes spoke again when he had the cigarette burning.

'How are you going to manage your paper round, now that you're here with us, Mr. Maguire?'

'Oh, I gave it up last night, sir.'

When he looked at me he seemed a bit surprised.

'Why?'

'Well, sir, the job here in the office has to come first. I know that if I'm going to get on I'm going to have to work hard. I want to be able to concentrate on insurance and I hope to get into the Technical School in Rathmines very shortly.'

After that mouthful I took a deep breath, only hoping that I hadn't gone too far with the bullshit. He looked a bit puzzled again. He couldn't figure me out. But then it was Redmond and me that he was up against, which was a different matter altogether. He was a man who thought the best of everyone and I felt a bit of a louse to be telling him all those lies, but there was nothing else I could do. If I told him the truth about losing the job because Cahill and his chatty pal had kept me over an hour late that would be knocking the manager on my first day in the office and I couldn't see that as being a clever thing to do. Anyway, with all the scheming that I'd had to keep a tanner in my pocket it was almost impossible for me not to slip a lie in here and there.

'The firm would pay for evening classes,' Mr. Hayes said. 'Going to school after work is the way a lot of people have to do it and it's not a bad way.'

'Thank you, sir,' I said. 'That's more than I ever expected,' and I thought to myself, Jeysus, you're not kidding.

Before the interview finished, Mr. Hayes told me to come and see him if I was in doubt about anything, that he would always be willing to help me if he could do so. And you could tell that he meant what he said.

Larry Deegan was still at his desk when I finished the post. Cahill put on his hat and coat and went out without so much as a good night. I couldn't understand how anyone could get to be that kind of a pig, but whatever it was that was needed Cahill had got more than his share of it. I was tying up the bundle of letters when Larry came up the office.

'Do you drink, Paddy?'

I grinned at him.

'Does a fish swim?'

We walked down to College Green together and I shoved the letters into the post box. Then we walked up into Grafton Street to this little pub that Larry used. He didn't seem the least bit surprised that I took a drink and later on he told me that he'd started on the gargle as early as fourteen. He was from out of town and all those kids start to drink early. I suppose there's nothing else to do but drink or play with yourself.

He bought a round of Guinness and I told him that I wasn't all that flush, which was true enough. I had about three bob which would buy a few drinks, but you wouldn't be able to go mad on it. He wasn't bothered, he'd had a few quid off the horses and he fancied a good shant so, as he said, if you wanted to have a drink with a fella and he wasn't carrying it didn't matter. Next time it might be the other way round. Anyway, he said, you could always pay back by buying a drink for somebody else. That way it went around, and time was a great leveller.

'What do you make of the office?'

He gave me a cigarette and when I lit it I made sure not to swallow the smoke. Last time I'd done that I'd been sick all day. I didn't care all that much for smoking, anyway, but it was an American cigarette and at that time I was crazy about anything American. It must have had something to do with all those cowboy pictures I'd been looking at all those years.

'I like the office,' I said, 'but I'd like it even better if that bastard Cahill wasn't there.'

After I'd said it I wondered if I hadn't been stupid. I mean, I didn't really know Larry and it wasn't smart to shoot off your mouth to just anybody. Larry seemed to read my mind.

'Don't worry about saying that to me. I couldn't agree with

you more if I was getting paid for it.' He dragged deep on the cigarette. 'Thing is, though, not to let him bother you. He's just not that important, he's not even intelligent. Let's face it, a well-trained Alsatian could do his job. He's just a bug, a tiny little bug, a peasant with a mind the size of a threepenny stamp, and he uses his little bit of authority to take it out on people who are in no position to answer back.'

He picked up his glass and drank deep. As far as he was concerned, Cahill was for the birds, and that night we didn't mention his name again. I drank some of the stout and I made myself a promise not to let Cahill get my back up any more. As Larry said, he was just a little snot and he wasn't worth the energy that I was prepared to waste on him. When I emptied the glass and put it down on the table it struck me that Larry had the same name as my kid brother who'd died that time with the consumption, and that made me double glad we were friends.

For the rest of the week I didn't see much of Larry. He was down in County Meath trying to sell insurance to an American film producer who'd bought himself a stud farm or something. Like most Yanks, he was also trying to find the little thatched cottage in the hills where his grandmother had been born and reared amongst the pigs and the chickens. And when he found out that she'd really been born in Brooklyn or Manhattan and had ended up as a French whore in the Bronx he'd ignore it and still go on looking in Ireland, the biggest shop window in America.

You could tell by the hum in the office that it was regarded as a big chance for the firm and for Larry. Cahill was bloody sarcastic about Larry's chances of succeeding, laughing at the very idea of a trainee handling such a job. But he was only choked that he hadn't gotten the chance. He liked the thought of the commission that might be in it.

The reason Larry was on it was because he'd made the contact himself through a cousin of his in the American Air Force. When he got back he told me that he'd clinched the deal on the Wednesday and spent the rest of the week as house guest to the Yank and his missus. And from the way he acted, although he didn't actually say anything, I got the feeling that he'd been a lot closer to the missus than he had to the producer. Not that it mattered, it was good to have him back and to see Cahill's margarine face go green when he heard that Larry had completed the business with no bother at all.

For a while after that Larry had a vague American accent and he wore a tie that the Yank had given him and it was so loud that you could have heard it round the corner. And he was talking about getting laid and about playing the ponies and the next time we went for a drink he ordered whiskey on the rocks and I thought he was a head case until I saw the lumps of ice in his glass.

While Larry had been away in County Meath I'd gotten to know some of the girls in the office a bit better. They were all okay, though some of them were a bit dozy, and then there was the one on the switch who was a cheeky cow that you couldn't help liking, and I was happier than ever in the job. And I'd had a smile from Maureen Murphy in the little broker's office and I couldn't get her out of my mind.

One of the girls in our place, Mary Whelan, was a great skin. She had a big fresh Galway face and she was very nice to me in a big sister sort of way. Her father was an inspector on the buses, which was a good job in Dublin, and she rode a bicycle with a cyclo-gear three-speed and my tongue nearly fell out with envy whenever I saw her ride it home to lunch. I mean, if you were seen on a bicycle like that you were really treated as somebody.

Liz O'Boyle was the one on the switchboard and not only was she cheeky but she was a right prick-teaser with it. There was another mot there, Maria Daly by name, and she tried to be nice to me. But God, when she leaned over the desk to ask me how I was getting on there was the most awful smell from her, and it was hard not to tell her straight out that she needed a bath. Every time she talked to me the others would be watching and they'd have a laugh among themselves, but not one of them ever told the girl. And how she went about her business without realising it herself was a mystery to me. She must have had a blockage in her nose or something, that's all I can say.

As I said, the other girls were all right, but none of them did anything for me, just nice heads of cabbage with powder and lipstick on. Well-shaped vegetables that beat words out of typewriters.

Friday lunchtime we were paid and I felt very grown-up to be getting my first-ever pay-packet. It was a small buff-coloured envelope with my name on it and when I opened it I found three small tickets inside as well as my wages and the pay slip. They were my admission tickets to the Technical School for Geography, Commerce and English classes. I filled up when I read the words and I truly felt a louse for lying to Mr. Hayes the way I did. I never expected anyone except Ma to care whether I lived or died. I was surprised and grateful and I had the tickets in my hand. I would use them. Mr. Hayes had made the first step for me. Now I'd show him that he hadn't made a bad investment. I'd work hard and get good reports, so that he'd know I was trying at least. It had started off as a lie but it wasn't going to end up that way.

When I counted the money there was thirty-five shillings. I checked it again and again to make sure I wasn't kidding myself. Then I looked at the slip. It said thirty-five shillings. I didn't know what to think.

Mr. Hayes called out for me to come in when I knocked at the door of his office. He was on the phone, but when he saw me he picked up a letter that was lying on the desk and handed it to me without a word. I left the office and stood outside to read it. It was confirmation that my wages were to be thirty-five shillings per week and not thirty as previously stated. It was all too much for me. I rushed out of the office and into the washroom. I went into an empty closet and I just let go. The tears burst out of me, like a pain out of my chest, and I slid down along the wall on to the floor. It just poured out. I couldn't have stopped it anyway. I was torn apart with kindness and nobody should ever get that out of touch. Kindness should never hurt anyone the way it did me that day.

But I knew that it was more than that. It was partly guilt that I felt for lying to Mr. Hayes. At the same time I knew that the tears wouldn't change anything. I'd had to scheme and connive for too long to be able to switch it off like a light just because I came up against someone who was really decent. And still I knew that out of thanks to him I'd try to be the fella he thought I was. It wouldn't be easy but I'd try.

Kindness was a quality that I didn't know much about. It's not something that blossoms in a jungle like The Hill, where ignorance and superstition and violence and hatred fester in each other's arms like sores.

I suppose Mrs. Kearney was kind, but she had her reasons. I got a few shillings and a meal and a drink out of her and she had given me my first pair of long trousers, but she expected payment. Skinny and all as I was, she expected payment. No, the only really kind person I'd ever known before Mr. Hayes was Ma. If she had a fault it was that her heart was as big as her body. She was kindness and she was love.

7

BEFORE I left the lavatory I scrubbed the face off myself to try and hide my red eyes. And I filled a basin with hot water, dipping my hankie into it and pressing it against my eyes like a poor man's hot towel. By the time I'd finished I didn't look too bad and I didn't feel too bad either. A good weep relieves the pressure, at least it does for me. I've never been ashamed to cry. I just wouldn't want to be the type who bottles it up. If something's got to come out of your system it might as well come out through your eyes. It's not so hard that way.

Back in the office, Cahill gave me a hard look. He was telling me not to be so bloody long in the future, but he didn't say anything. I tidied up my desk and did a bit of filing. Then I copied a proposal form, which brought me up to lunchtime, and I had plenty to think about on the way home in the bus.

That extra five shillings a week in my pay-packet. What was I going to do about it? Ma thought, as I had done myself until an hour ago, that I would be earning thirty shillings a week. Should I talk to her about it? Should I offer it to her? It was a difficult thing to decide just like that, so I kept my mouth shut. I needed a little time to think.

It was fish and chips from the fish shop for lunch and when I got in Billy was already dug into his share. Josie wasn't there. She worked over the north side of the city and it was too far for her to come home for lunch. I didn't mind that, the less I saw of her the better I liked it.

When Billy went out to the bog to read *The Independent* I asked Ma if twenty-five shillings a week would be okay for her. She poured me a cup of tea and sat down facing me.

'That won't leave you all that much, will it?'

'Ah, I'll have enough, Ma. You know me, I can always pick a shilling up here and there.'

She smiled and it was good to see. Since she'd lost Larry it wasn't often that she smiled. I don't think she ever got over him dying like that.

'I'd like to buy a bike with the pocket money, Ma. Is that okay with you?'

'Oh, I don't know, son, getting into all that debt just for a bicycle. It's not an easy thing to pay out every week.'

'I know, Ma,' I said, 'but sure I'll be spending it all on bus fares, anyway. If I had a bike I could get another paper round just for the mornings. That'd help pay for it and I'd be able to go for a ride on a Sunday. I'd love to get one, Ma.'

'How much do you have to put down?'

'Only a pound. I saw a poster in a shop in Aungiers Street and it said a pound deposit would be enough. Can I get one?'

She nodded her head and I jumped up and ran round the table and kissed her on the face.

'Where'll you get the pound deposit?'

'Ah, I'll save it up. A couple of months and I should have it. I won't use the bus, I'll walk up and down to save the fare.'

She knew I didn't mean it and I knew that she knew, and she knew that I knew she knew. It was a game and she was being just as wicked as I was. We both knew that I was after the pound out of my first week's pay-bag and she smiled as though she was calling me a right crafty little bastard.

'You can use the pound out of your wages today,' she said, and you could feel the pleasure she got from being able to give. God, I had to work awful hard not to tell her about that extra five shillings!

'Ah, thanks a million, Ma. You're sure that the twenty-five a week'll be okay for you?'

She nodded happily and I didn't feel so bad. If she was happy with twenty-five shillings then what I had for myself didn't enter into it. Anyway, one pound five a week wasn't bad for a fella of my age to be bringing home, no matter what he was earning. It really wasn't, I told myself, and I kept on at it until I was absolutely convinced that I was a great fella to be giving the mother that much. And when I thought about the other dollar from Mrs. Kearney I felt rich. Things were going just fine and I'd keep on going up to see her as long as she kept her promise, though it was getting harder and harder to fancy her since I'd seen Maureen Murphy and her yellow sweater.

Saturday lunchtime I walked up to the bicycle shop in Aungiers Street to get the form for the hire purchase. I got an awful drop when the oul' fella told me I'd have to get someone to go guarantee for me in case I got tired making the payments. That was something I hadn't even thought about. Jeysus, I could have kicked myself for being so empty-headed, and anyway, who in the name of Christ was going to guarantee me for anything except maybe a stretch in Mountjoy Jail?

I could ask Mrs. Kearney, but that might somehow mess up my chances of getting the dollar a week out of her and I couldn't risk that. Mr. Hayes had said he'd help me any way he could, but even with my hard neck I couldn't ask him. Then I thought about Larry Deegan. He was a great fella and he wasn't a worrier over money and I felt that he'd tell me straight out, yes or no, with no excuses. Larry wasn't the kind of fella to make a song and a dance out of anything. So I decided, even though I knew it was an awful cheek, to ask him on Monday morning.

When I got home I told Ma that I'd put the pound down on the bike, just in case she'd changed her mind, and I tried hard to forget the bike for the rest of the weekend. I didn't succeed. When you want something as badly as I wanted to have a bicycle of my own, it's right in front of your bloody eyes even when you're asleep.

The Stella was favourite on Sunday afternoon. The film started about three, so that if you had an early lunch you had time for a good few drinks before the picture. And with most of the shows they'd been getting in recent months you needed a few drinks to sit through them. I was well known around The 'Mines and there was always somebody to hold a place for me in the queue. Usually, when I crept in and started chatting to the fella, some oul' one behind would start slagging me for not taking my turn and I used to turn on the Blarney. And if that didn't work I'd just turn a deaf ear and act as though she wasn't there. You had to be careful all the same. Some of them oul' ones'd give you a right-hander, which didn't do you any good, because no matter how badly you might want to thump one of them, you couldn't.

Inside the cinema you never sat more than three rows from the back. There was always a load of mots that were on the look-out for a good neck and a grope and it's no exaggeration to say that they rarely went home disappointed. And to look at them outside in the queue you wouldn't think butter would melt in their mouths.

When you got one of them in the back row, though, you knew it wasn't your sister. And it wasn't just the odd one either, there was no scarcity at all. Publicans' daughters, policemen's daughters, girls from all over the Rathmines and Rathgar and Terenure, girls that wouldn't talk to you if they knew you came from a place like The Hill. But they didn't know, they didn't even know your name, and they forgot their class consciousness, anyway, and opened their brassières for you in the darkness of the back row of The Stella.

There are people in Dublin who wouldn't and couldn't and can't accept this. Apart from the scruff from the slums, our girls are all virgins until they go to their wedding beds. They believe in the Commandments of God and they listen to their priests. Maybe they do, but in the privacy of a cinema with only a thousand people in it they forget exactly what it was the priest has said, and they remember only that they want to touch and be touched and to get as much out of it as they can. Girls are girls and boys will be boys, but it only takes two to tango.

Sunday mornings now, I did one of two things. I left the house in time for eleven Mass. I didn't ever want Ma to find out that I hadn't been in a church since the day Larry was buried. And I went either for a walk along The Dodder or I took a bus into town. If I went to town I always went to the same ice-cream parlour in Grafton Street and I had a long jar of cream and mixed fruit and chocolate syrup. It was cold and it helped to fix my stomach after the Guinness of the night before. I loved it too. At half a crown a time ice-cream and fruit was a luxury, it was really living.

I couldn't go to Mass or Confession. I didn't believe in it and I couldn't accept anything about the whole set-up. I'm not knocking religion. It's not important enough for me to kick it. It was just that I couldn't take it and I felt even more that way since Larry had died. I felt too that if there was a God, and I didn't really think so for one minute, then he would in his glory and his omnipotence and all the rest of it understand what made me feel the way I did. And if he didn't want to know, then good luck to him, for all I cared. But for Ma's sake I shammed at being a Catholic. Sooner or later I was bound to break her heart and I just wanted to postpone it as long as I could.

That particular Sunday night I went to The Mansion House, to a one and sixpenny ceilidhe. It was my first dance and I only went because Redmond, believe it or not, and a fella called Tooler Doogan talked me into it.

We were having a drink in The Bleeding Horse, near the old Camden Cinema, where the screen was behind you when you went in the door, and I was contented to stay there and get on

72

with the drinking. And I couldn't have been in better company from the point of view of hard drinking. Doogan was as good at dropping pints as Redmond was, and, as he said himself, 'Boy, I'd drink porter off a dead soldier's arse.' Anyway, when the Mansion House was suggested for a change I said all right. The way I was feeling I'd have gone on a camping trip to the Dublin Mountains right there and then.

Redmond had been before, which came as a surprise to me. He always seemed so tired and lazy that I'd never dreamed of him doing 'The Walls of Limerick' or 'The Haymaker's Jig'. And yet when I thought about it it made sense. For an admission fee of one and sixpence he could have a dance and chat to as many mots as he liked, and with it being all Irish dancing the chances were that most of the lassies would be country girls. And it was a safe bet that half of them would be in domestic work, which was right up Redmond's alley.

He was all on to go and I felt so good in my new suit, and all that stout inside me had me feeling game for anything. Doogan said then that it was a great place for getting a leave home and that mots of all ages went there.

'Just as well, isn't it?' I said to Redmond.

'How do you mean?' he said, falling in.

'Well, if there were only young ones there there wouldn't be any use in you going, now would there?'

He burst out laughing, refusing to bite any further. 'Listen to it, will you, Tooler, trying to kid a fella who's kidded thousands!'

We chipped in and took a cab over to Dawson Street, and though I wouldn't have let Redmond know it I was thrilled to be going to a dance. It was something new and I was dying to see what The Round Room was like.

It really was a round room and there was an eight-hand reel going on when we got in there. The dancers were hopping about, innocent-looking people, dancing for the sake of dancing, if their expressions were anything to go by. But still, I thought,

73

you can never tell. Sometimes a fella had to act with a mot, even when he's dancing.

There was a big crowd and it seemed from the atmosphere that everyone was having a good time. Even the band, who were working their nuts off, looked happy, and it felt good just to be there. The next dance was 'The Siege of Ennis' and when Redmond shuffled off to get himself a partner I stood back beside Doogan. The next thing Harry comes back with three mots and he gave one to myself and Doogan, as though they were cigarettes. I tried to get out of the dance, but he wouldn't hear of it.

'What's your name, macushla?' he asked the girl who was to be my partner.

'Nuala Ryan,' she said in a soft lilting voice.

'Good girl, Nuala,' said Redmond, in his Trinity College voice. 'This chap here is Paddy Maguire, son of the famous and sometimes notorious Eamonn Óg, but as this is his first time to a dance he's a bit shy, despite his heritage. Will you give him the pleasure of your company in this dance?'

She nodded, just a little bit overwhelmed by Redmond's mouthful, and when I looked from her to Tooler Doogan, I could see from the amazement on his face that he wasn't as used to Harry as I was.

'Right,' said Redmond, giving the other girl to Doogan as though there was no need for further explanation, 'come on then. We'll get into the same set and you just follow me.'

The girl gave me her hand and I followed Redmond on to the dance floor, with Doogan and his partner behind me. We had to stand for a minute while things got organised, those Irish dances take a few minutes to get under way, and while we did I had a chance for a good look at my partner.

She was nearly my height, which was tall for a girl, and she was slim with apple breasts. Her hair was black and she had clear blue eyes and if she'd had a decent hair-do and a bit of make-up on she'd have been a real looker. She smiled at me and her eyes were kind. She was probably a civil servant. Apart from anything else, you could tell by the softness of her hands that she wasn't a kitchen mechanic, and it was a safe bet that someday she'd make some fella very happy. I liked her and I was grateful to her for being so nice.

The men stood in a line facing the girls and then the dance began. Redmond was marvellous, not just a clod-hopper like most of the fellas in the room, including Doogan. And while he danced he kept up a non-stop patter act to his partner and she never stopped laughing at him.

I hopped as well as I could and thanks to the Guinness I wasn't the least bit shy. It was really enjoyable and I was sorry when it came to an end. I learned something too, people who won't get up and dance because they think others are going to be looking at them are just kidding themselves. Most people are too busy enjoying themselves to bother about whether a fella can dance or not.

A bit later I did a 'Walls of Limerick', which is probably the easiest Irish dance of them all. I copied Redmond and found that I was moving well and the girls were all nice. Honestly, if you made a wrong move nobody pulled a face or did anything to make you feel a fool. It was hard on the legs, though, and when it finished I went up to the balcony to have a sit down.

Doogan was already up there, sitting drinking orange with a mot who was a pot-walloper if ever I saw one. And a few minutes later Redmond came up with a woman of about forty. She was thickly built and she had a nervous laugh that I could hear three seats away, but Redmond was looking at her as though she was Greta Garbo. He sat down, giving me a wink and cocking his arm with the fist closed behind her back. I smiled and shook my head. There was no stopping that Redmond. He mightn't have been the best-looking fella in the place, but when he put on the charm he could work wonders with the women.

He sat with his back to me and in a minute he was kissing her as if they were married. She was pushing him away and looking to see that nobody was watching them, but you could see that she was lapping it up. Then he said something to her and she nodded. Next thing they were getting up from the table and she was going downstairs. He walked over to where I was sitting and leaned over the table, a grin on his crooked mouth.

'I'm baling out now, kid. Off to do my good deed for the day.'

'With your woman?'

'Yeh, she's a widow and from the way she trembles when you get near her nobody's sunk the log there in recent months, so I'm going to give her one. See you in the week. So long.'

And he was gone down the stairs after her, away to make urgent love to the well-built widow and the behind of his trousers shining like a new pair of patent-leather shoes.

I went home shortly afterwards, tired and a bit nervous about the morning. For all the drink and the fun the bike was still at the head of my thoughts, and while I honestly didn't for one minute think that Larry would turn me down, I still felt it was a lot to ask of a fella that you'd only known for such a short time.

Monday morning, when I woke up, I was still thinking about the bike and the difference it could make to my life. I could get another paper round for mornings only. It would be easy to do with a bike of my own. And the pay for that would near enough cover the weekly instalments. On weekends, as I said to Ma, I'd be able to go off somewhere for a spin if I wanted to. The mountains and the seaside were very handy to Dublin and there were plenty of mots about who would wear you like a glove if you had a bike. I even imagined myself giving a crossbar to Maureen Murphy and her skirt blew up and I saw the tops of her legs and she had a yellow sweater on.

Larry came over to me for a chat at tea break and I asked him straight out if he'd go guarantor for me. I liked him too much to try and chat him into it, and anyway he was too smart a fella to wear that kind of an approach. He didn't even ask me how much the bike was or what the repayments were. He just took the form and signed it where the oul' fella in the shop had marked it with a cross in pencil. And when I tried to thank him he shrugged and brought his hands up like wings from his chest.

'Forget it, will you?'

So I left it at that, knowing that any further talk about it would only embarrass him.

Ten days later I threw my leg over the crossbar for the first time and if it had been Trigger, instead of a Humber bicycle with twenty-two-inch wheels and a four-and-sixpenny lamp, I couldn't have been happier or more excited. The oul' fella in the shop was a bit snotty with me, telling me to take it easy and all the rest of it. You could see he thought I was too young to have a bike of my own, even though he was making a few quid out of the deal. Still, if he'd been the Lord Mayor of Dublin, I couldn't have cared less about him, but I did think that the oul' turd strangler might have had the common decency to wish me luck.

Like a king, that's how I felt as I rode up Aungiers Street, the bike solid as a rock under me. It was a gift to ride, especially after that heavy thing that I'd had to ride in the butcher's shop. There was nothing that could harm me and there wasn't anyone that could shoot me down. I was a royal figure as I rode past the fish-dealers at their stalls and I went through Charlemont Street, tall and strong in the saddle and I didn't give twopenny worth of cold spit for anybody. God, it was a wonderful feeling, the likes of which a fella doesn't feel many times in his life.

Near the tennis club on Ranelagh Road I caught up with Noggler Green, and I got a shock when I saw that he didn't have a three-speed on his bicycle any more. It may seem strange that I noticed that so quickly, but not when you think of how crazy

. ...s about bicycles. And Noggler had always had a good machine. Whenever you passed the little house that he lived in on Charleston Road you'd see him polishing it. At one time I was worried that he'd rub the paint off it. Honestly, he never left it alone. Now to see him without the three-speed was like seeing him without his cap on and that was something I couldn't even have imagined.

'Hello, Mr. Green.'

I was riding beside him and he turned his weary peak-capped head to look at me, and his watery eyes were like wet overcoat buttons.

'Hello, Paddy,' he sniffed. 'Got yourself a machine?'

'Yeh,' I nodded, 'but what happened to your three-speed, Mr. Green?'

'I took it off,' he said, and you'd think he was talking about his vest or his shirt the way he said it.

'But why, Mr. Green?'

I half expected him to tell me to mind my own bloody business but, Jeysus, when someone took a three-speed off a bike you had to try and find out why.

'It slipped the other day when I was pushing up over the Charlemont Bridge. I nearly smashed me testicles.'

'Your what, Mr. Green?'

'Me testicles, me ballocks,' he said, a pain coming into his face. 'Bloody thing nearly ruptured me.'

'Oh,' I said, nearly pissing myself. 'That's no joke.'

'Too bloody true it's not,' he said in disgust, and the look on his leathery face was just grey misery. Then he was gone along to the left towards Ranelagh, mumbling to himself about 'the only bitta pleasure that's left to us' and I made off to the right and up the hill that led to the flats. And I was wondering if it would have made any difference to him if he had damaged his nuts. I couldn't for the life of me see him getting on the job, not Noggler. He looked more like an oul' fella who'd rather have a cup of sugary tea than a slice off the legs, but then as Redmond had proved by going to The Mansion House on that Sunday night you can never be sure about people.

Ma blushed with pleasure when she saw the bicycle and I think that all the oul' ones in the block must have come down to wish me luck and to have a screw at it. Except oul' Darcy, with her mouth on her like a torn pocket, starting on about how dangerous the roads were and all the rest of it. God, I could willingly have put my fist in her face. Ma was a big enough worrier without getting something fresh to start on.

Billy didn't say a word about the bike. Not that he was jealous or anything like that, he just wasn't interested. He liked clothes and white shirts and he was always as neat as a well-washed corpse. And if he'd had a new suit I wouldn't have said anything about that, so him keeping his mouth shut about the bike was fair enough I suppose.

8

GOING to work on the bike made life sweeter for me and even having to return to The Hill didn't seem so bad.

I used to ride up and down singing my head off, not in the least put out by the way people looked at me. Honest, the way some of them used to gape you'd think I was giving them a flash of the john thomas or something. I felt so happy that I just didn't care and even when the rain poured down on me I'd end up singing 'Singing in the Rain'.

By the end of that first week I'd found a new paper round which paid ten bob for six mornings' work. This was marvellous, because the money covered the payment for the bike and I could still have a lie-in on Sunday morning. There were a good few papers to be delivered each day, but I shot round and seemed to get them all finished in no time.

It's funny when you think about it, but regardless of the really full day I was putting in I started two nights a week in Rathmines Technical School as well. That was one of my happiest times. One night I did the geography and commerce classes and the other night I took English.

From the off the Tech was great. Not in the least bit like the National School, with the endless Irish and the beatings every time you looked crooked. And being older and fairly well dressed, and having a bike and a job that I liked doing, helped no end. Also there were girls in the classes, some of them even sitting beside you at the desk, and though this didn't help the concentration much, it was very nice all the same.

I was determined as I could be to learn something from those classes, so each night I went right up to the front row and made it my business to listen to what the teachers were on about. I suppose it was the fact that I didn't have to go that made it so enjoyable, it was free and easy. You could tell that if you didn't show up one night, the teacher couldn't have cared less. It was the sort of attitude that I liked. You know, like as if you were free, although it was this very thing that made you go regularly and get more involved than you could ever have done at the National School.

The English teacher was the one I liked best. He was a right comedian and he had this way of saying things that just made you want to hear more. He was a tall fella with a sort of bevelled face that went in from the forehead and worked its way out gradually by the time it reached his chin. And he kept taking his glasses off and putting them back on again and he wasn't past giving the eye to one or two of the mots. You could see that if he had one of them on her own he wouldn't be too concerned about her bad grammar.

In the commerce class they tried to teach you to write business letters in a more modern style than we beg to acknowledge and all that rubbish. I made notes and listened carefully. I thought of Cahill. His letters were about as modern as the pictures Mack Sennett used to make with Ben Turpin and all that mob. All the old corny clichés were for ever getting slung into his correspondence and when he said something like 'with particular reference to your penultimate paragraph' or 'this man was the author of his own misfortune' he looked as if he'd just pulled the phrase right out of the air. I could see that if I followed the line that the Tech people wanted to teach, Cahill and I were going to be at each other's throats sooner or later.

I was really interested in the geography class too. I was a

right head case, I know, but I cared about how much carboniferous limestone was in one country and how much rain fell annually in another. Facts like that just fascinated me. The teacher built up pictures of strange places with fabulous names, and I'd sit there dreaming of Java and Peru, and I was crazy to get down and see the Virgin Isles, though to be perfectly honest I was more interested in the birds that lived there, thinking they must all be virgins and dying for it on account of the shortage of men. As I say, I was a right header. I couldn't help thinking of crumpet even though I did want to learn something. Let's face it, I needed to learn something, for it was there in the Technical School that I discovered that Egypt was in Africa. I think above all else that this illustrates just how much I didn't learn at the National School.

Thanks to the English class I was becoming aware of names in the world of literature . . . Maugham, Steinbeck, Thomas Wolfe. And when the teacher mentioned William Butler Yeats I smiled, thinking of all the unfortunate kitchen mechanics and pot-wallopers that Redmond had bullshitted to up on the Dodder banks.

'What do you do, Harry?' said the big one from Galway.

'Me . . . ah, I'm a writer . . . a poet . . . you know.' The hand worked its way up under her jumper and on to bare flesh that never knew the feel of a support. Then the recitation as he worked the knee between easy thighs, token resistance, the words tumbling out of his crooked mouth. Yeats and Wordsworth and the others opening the legs for him. His return to the boozer and the details of the ride and his own brand of poetry through the Guinness and the laughter that rocked him where he sat. 'I gave her tits a little suck, and the cheeks of her arse, went chuck chuck chuck!

Maugham impressed me then. I envied him the English that dripped from his fingertips and he told a good yarn. Steinbeck I loved for *The Grapes of Wrath*. I cried for his people and I admired his great humility. And Thomas Wolfe for his near-great *Look Homeward Angel*. The bits of this that I couldn't understand did worry me, but I hadn't anybody that I could ask about them. I didn't know one person who cared a damn about writers or the things they wrote. Not a solitary soul could I talk to about my reading. The teacher, I felt, would be willing enough. He'd loaned me the books that I've mentioned, but he had his job to do with the class. Even Redmond, who was brilliant in his own way, would have laughed at me if I'd tried to talk literature with him. For weeks and weeks I was burning up with frustration, not knowing what the hell I could do about it.

So, because I couldn't talk to anybody, I began to write things down. I didn't think of it as writing, it was just me talking to myself on paper. Nobody ever saw the stuff I wrote. It was mine, conversation through the tip of my pen, and it made me a whole lot happier. So much so that I stopped even looking for someone to talk to about books and writers. I was talking to myself now and that was enough.

I enjoyed the physical thing of writing. For hours and hours I'd sit in the reading room of the library next door to the Tech, and I'd scribble away, filling exercise books one after the other. I couldn't have done this at home, the radio was on most of the time. If not that, Billy listened to popular records on his new pick-up and if I was there I sat and listened and loved every second of it, even though I felt it was a waste of time. So the reference room became my study and I spent lots of time there, just reading and writing and dreaming a bit too.

I remember the day that I got my hands on a copy of *The Great Gatsby*. I didn't know the book, but I'd seen the film with Alan Ladd in it. A bloody terrible picture, but I thought it might help me understand the book. As it happened it was a marvellous book, probably one of the greatest, and when I thought about the lousy picture they'd made of it I bled for Scott Fitzgerald. I read that book three times in a month and I never tired of it for one second.

It taught me something too. For a book to be great it didn't have to be full of big words and all kinds of vague references to Greek mythology and all the rest of it. People like Fitzgerald proved that, and I got the feeling that he wanted every man on earth to be able to read his book, to be able to share the experience that his genius had forced on to the paper. And I knew that I wouldn't be afraid to pick up a book any more. If there were words that I didn't know I'd use a dictionary to find the meaning. I wanted to learn, so I'd go on reading and I'd continue scribbling into the exercise books and someday I'd learn how to type and I'd work and slave to become a writer. The start of a dream that never died, although more than once it got shoved aside because of a mot with overgrown mammary glands or a pint of Guinness with a nice white collar on it.

Maureen Murphy didn't help. She was responsible for a long delay in me getting on with the writing, and to think the poor girl never knew how close she was to the fella who someday was going to set the world alight with his stories. I used to stand in the middle of the road, carried away by the sight of my book topping best-seller lists all over the world. And I won every prize ever awarded for fiction-writing and the miracle of it all was that I never got run down by a bus or something for my stupid day dreaming.

I was just about to sling the English class when Maureen arrived one night. Writers and their books had been left behind and there was all kinds of chat about grammar and syntax and that kind of stuff. I wasn't interested. I had neither eye nor ear for transitive verbs and conjunctions and split infinitives. To me it was more simple, I looked at something and it was right or wrong and at that time I felt that this was enough. So I was fed-up and wanted to get back to books themselves and when I knew that this wouldn't happen for ages I was about to bale out. Then, as I say, Maureen arrived and things seemed different.

When she walked into the classroom ahead of me I could hardly believe it. I mean, I was a king among dreamers. In my over active imagination I'd done the lot and done it very well too. Yet I'd never for one second considered the possiblity that she might show up in the Tech, And, believe me, that was a damn' sight more likely than the most ordinary things I dreamed up all the time.

She really was a lovely little girl, and, God, when I looked at her the heart started pumping the chest off me. I still saw her most days on delivery and I talked all sorts of cobblers to her about weather and the like, but cheeky and all as I was I just couldn't find the courage to ask her for a date. I was crazy about her, but when I got near her I could only talk about nothing.

That night, though, I was determined to do something about her, so when she sat down I moved into the desk beside her before I could stop and think about it. If I did that I knew I'd never make a move.

'Hello there.'

She looked up at me with her blue eyes. She was very sure of herself.

'What are you doing here?' she smiled.

I could only shrug, hardly knowing what to say.

'Just trying to pick up a few things.'

She looked about the classroom, then back to me.

'There's plenty here,' she said, and her eyes sparkled with devilment.

I grinned, but I could feel my face go red. I knew she was having me on, but I wanted to tell her that it was only herself that I was interested in. She looked older than she did in the office, she might have been twenty, and I wondered if I looked old enough even to be talking to her.

'Trying to learn something,' I said.

85

'I didn't think you were the type,' The teacher had arrived and he got up on his platform. Maureen took a couple of pencils from her handbag and she put them in front of her on the desk. I noticed that her hands were trembling ever so slightly and it wasn't cold in the room. I wanted to think that I was making her nervous, but I was afraid to believe it. If I was wrong, and she snuffed me out like a candle, which she could have done, I wouldn't be able to do a thing about it.

That evening I didn't hear a word that the teacher said. I wasn't able to concentrate. My insides were all tight and I had a pain in my neck and shoulders from the effort of not looking at her all the time. Once or twice I had the feeling that she was looking at me, but I still couldn't turn my head to see if she was. And I'll tell you one thing, I was never so pleased to get to the end of the class. I was worn out and all I'd been doing was sit there and not hear a bloody word.

We hadn't spoken either through the lesson and when we got out on the Rathmines Road, still somehow together, I was dreading the second when she was going to walk away from me. If someone had told me that I could be that stupid I'd have laughed in his face. I was a big-chat merchant, I could talk to anybody. Even Ma used to make the old joke about me being vaccinated with a gramophone needle.

'It gets dark early, doesn't it?' Maureen said.

'Yeh, it does. Still, the summer'll soon be here and it'll be a bit lighter in the evenings.'

We stood there looking at each other and a load of kids came running by. Like whippets they were, bumping into everyone as they flashed along the footpath. They were screaming about the picture they had just seen in The Prinner. Scruffy little urchins without an arse in their trousers and it stopped me dead to see them. Only yesterday it was, Larry and me kicked out by the gunner-eyed attendant. Little Larry, God love him, the night he ruined his trousers and Ma had to wash him all over before he went to bed. I felt sick with myself. That was the first thought of him in so long. Nothing was fixed and sure. Everything faded. Only the ground that you finally went into was the same. Only the earth endured. . . .

'Can I give you a crossbar home, Maureen?'

'I didn't know you had a bike.'

Before I could say anything this big-mouth came along the path pushing a Raleigh Lenten Clubman with one hand. It had a three-speed and dynohub on it and all the other extras that cost so much, and he swaggered as though he owned the whole neighbourhood. He was about nineteen or twenty, a fairly big fella with a high forehead and straight black hair split on one side. He was good-looking, I suppose, but he had a mean mouth and there was no denying that he thought he was the cream off the milk.

'Hey, Maureen, come on an' I'll walk you home.' He said it as though he was doing her a favour and he looked at me as though I'd just dropped out of a dog's arse.

'Where have you been?' she asked him, and the way she smiled hurt me more than a kick in the nuts would have done.

'Playing snooker,' he grinned. 'Won two quid. Come on an' I'll buy you a Knickerbocker Glory.'

Shag you and your two quid and your Knickerbocker Glory head on you. I cursed him in my heart. Two quid was more than I earned in a whole week at the office. I no longer thought I didn't like him, I was sure I didn't.

'This is Paddy Maguire.' Maureen turned to me then. 'This is Willie Egan, the biggest chancer in Rathmines.'

I held out my hand. 'How do you do.'

He nodded his head, but he didn't say anything, and he made no attempt to shake my hand. I was wild to have put myself in such a position. I should have let him make the first move. I should have guessed that the bastard would have tried to make me look silly. Then I remembered all the times Redmond had said that fellas who tried to make you look stupid only did it because they were jealous of you, and though I couldn't see how that was the case I was more than willing to believe it.

'Well, are you comin' or not?'

She shook her head at him. 'I can't, I have a date with Paddy.'

I didn't look at her in case the surprise showed in my face, but I looked at him and I didn't mind that he hadn't taken my hand. Who needed him, anyway?

'My bike's around Leinster Road,' I said to Maureen.

She put her small hand into the crook of my arm and I looked at your man again. I'll say this for him, he didn't seem all that bothered and I knew that if it had been me I'd have been looking for a hole to crawl into.

'Good night, Willie.'

He grinned the way Douglas Fairbanks did just before he dived into the moat in *The Prisoner of Zenda*, and then he jumped up on the bike right there on the footpath. 'I'll see you around,' he said, and he shot off like a bullet and in a few seconds all we could see was the red hum of his rear reflector as he hit the top of Rathmines Road.

'He's an awful boaster,' Maureen said as we turned the corner into Leinster Road.

She didn't know then and I never told her how much she had helped me that night. To have backed me up when that bastard had tried to shoot me right up the arse was the biggest favour she could have done me. I was sick with the inferiority thing, one of the scars that you were sure to carry if you were born and lived on The Hill. I knew it even then and I hated myself for wallowing in self-pity, but I couldn't do a thing about it. Why me? I used to ask myself. Why couldn't I have been born in a decent house with a father who had a steady job, and so on. And when people rejected me I blamed it on the fact that they knew I was from The Hill. It never occurred to me that they mightn't have liked me anyway. I was sick with it, like I said, and I knew it and whether I could or not, at that time, I didn't try to do anything about it.

I wanted to tell her, there and then, how much I loved her and I think I could have done. The silent painful bit was over, I knew that from the way I felt, but I was afraid I'd frighten her off. So I kept quiet and we walked up the road and she held on to my arm. After a minute I took a deep breath and I moved my arm so that her hand fell free.

'What's the matter, Paddy?'

'I want to hold your hand.'

She put her small white hand in mine and the touch of it was an electric shock and I loved her and I wanted to die on the spot.

'You're a nice fella, aren't you?' She smiled up at me.

'It isn't difficult to be nice to you.'

Well, we were talking, anyway, even it it was a bit strained. The street was dark except where the street lights were, and when we turned into the lane that led up to Mount Drummond it was like the inside of an ink bottle. And still I wouldn't have been surprised if birds had started to chirp along the way.

We stopped without a word being said by a deep garage door-way and I put the bike against the wall. Maureen stood looking up at me and I put the bike against the wall. Like a magnet, she came against me and I kissed her with every bit of feeling and energy that was in me. Her hands went around the back of my neck and she held on to me and her breasts against me were hot pains in my miserable chest.

When she pulled away she looked at me and despite the dark-ness I could see that she couldn't believe what was happening and it was then that I knew she felt the way I did.

'I'm crazy about you, Maureen. Will you come out with me?'

She nodded without a word, and then pressing against me she tucked her head into my shoulder and I thought that I knew what it was to be really happy for the first time in my life.

'I haven't had a single date since the first day you came into our office,' she said. 'I want to go with you.'

'I'd like to go with you too, but I haven't the money or anything, like your man with the sports bike has.'

There it was again. It wasn't enough that this lovely girl wanted to be with me. I practically had to get it in writing.

She touched my face with her soft gentle hand. 'That doesn't matter to me,' she laughed. 'I don't like Knickerbocker Glorys, anyway.'

We both laughed at that and then suddenly, as if it had been cut with a knife, it stopped, and we were kissing again and I knew that I would love her for ever and ever.

Holding hands was different on the rest of the walk up to where she lived. It was like we'd been doing it for years and all the barriers that I'd forced between us, with my self-pity, were gone, and I knew that I'd never have any difficulty in speaking to her now.

She lived in a Corporation house with its own bathroom and I thought of how great it would have been if we'd moved there from The Hill when the houses were built a few years before. I kissed her again, lightly on her soft lips by the little iron gate.

'I love you,' she whispered, and then she was gone up the short concrete path and she went into the house without looking back.

That night the flats hit me worse than ever. On the way home I thought I'd burst with how I was feeling. Then just halfway up the lane it drained out of me and I felt cheated.

I got off the bike by the little huckster's shop and I stood for a minute looking in at the stale snow-cake and the pink fruit cake that usually had the flies all around it. A pot mender the size of a small saucer held the window together and I looked from that up the lane to the flats. It was still there, a sort of hopeless feeling, as if I was being sucked into something that I couldn't do anything about. I was choked with it. Even the way I felt about Maureen couldn't protect me from it. Happy as I'd been only minutes before, I was now as low as lino. I burned with my hate of the stinking place, hate for dirt and poverty and for pregnant paupers and for the Church that was the cause of the whole thing, and for the oul' fellas that held up the corners and for The Hill.

The dustbin in the corner of our hallway was smoking. Some lazy bastard had thrown a heap of burning cinders on top of the rubbish and I had to bite my teeth not to yell out and wake the whole block. Those bins had always been a curse, the brainchild of some prick in the Corporation. Very clever it was, an open bin in every hall, an open bin that stood where twenty-five men, women and mostly children had to pass in and out at all times. Mind you, I suppose the fact that there wasn't a lid of any kind did make it easier for the kids to fish the core of an apple out of the rubbish. I boiled all the time about it and I wasted more energy than I could afford while the people in the block slept. They accepted it without question. It had been put there by people in authority. That was enough.

I went into the flat, putting the bike against the scullery wall. There wasn't room for it, but you couldn't leave it outside for ten minutes, unless you wanted to get rid of it in a hurry. I was tired and depressed. I thought about making a drink of cocoa, but Ma was asleep in the bed in the kitchen with Josie, so I didn't bother about it.

Taking off my clothes in the dark of the bedroom I realised that I would have to get away from The Hill. No matter how long it took me or how hard it might be on Ma, I was going to have to get up and go. I loved Ma most of all, but when the right time came even that wouldn't stop me. I could feel it as I got into the bed and that made me more miserable than I already was.

9

From that night on I never got back to The Hill without hating it more and more and all the time. The need to go away from there was getting stronger and stronger. I'd stopped wondering how I'd feel if I left Ma and I couldn't imagine my life without blue-eyed Maureen, so as hard as I could I tried not to think about it. Love them both as I might, I couldn't lose the growing urge to get out. It was like a seed planted beneath concrete. It was there and it was pushing up out of the ground, and in time it would break through the crust that held it down.

Meanwhile I was happy in my work at the office and I was learning something all the time. Insurance is a very interesting business with something new cropping up nearly every day, and though I was only the office boy, and not doing much more than copying forms and doing the post, I was keeping my ears open, just dying for a chance to get stuck into the real thing. I wanted to be dictating letters and working out premiums and dealing with new clients at the counter. Business was on the increase all the time and I had the feeling that it wouldn't be too long at all before I'd get my chance.

Larry Deegan had an awful lot to do with the new business that was pouring in and he was making a bomb in commission. He was a natural-born salesman and he was lucky with it, always seeming to be in the right place at the right time. We were great pals now and with the way I was drinking with himself and Redmond I was building up a good head. It took more and more now to get me going. Mind you, most of the time I only drank Guinness. It was the right price for my pocket. At sevenpence or eightpence a bottle you could go a long way on ten bob or a pound. Whenever I drank spirits it was usually Larry who was paying.

I always enjoyed drinking with Larry. He was different to Redmond but in his own way just as interesting. He was a real person too, whereas Redmond was more of a character. Larry got on and did the things that Redmond told other people to do. He took life by the horns and twisted its neck. Redmond, I'd started to realise, was running away from life, using scivvies and pints of Guinness to escape from facing up to things.

Nothing surprised Larry. He knew all about Maureen and Mrs. Kearney and he howled at the idea of me doing all that loving in the house in Terenure. And the idea of me getting a dollar a week for it really appealed to him. You didn't have to be a choirboy or a religious maniac for Larry to think you were okay. He cared about people, despite what was wrong with them, accepting or rejecting people because of how they were, and not because of who they were or what they did in life.

He never said a word against Maureen, but I knew that he didn't think it was a good idea for a fella of my age to be going steady. He was against it on principle, feeling that you should enjoy every second of your single life because, he said, once you slipped that little gold band on a mot's finger you were buying sex on the hire purchase for the rest of your life. And I agreed with him, believing that he was dead right. Then I'd see Maureen and kiss her lips and no price seemed too high for the kick of just being with her.

It was true. For Maureen I was willing to do things that I wouldn't have done for anyone else. Like the Friday night we got to The Savoy Cinema in O'Connell Street. There was a queue a mile long and I gave it a very hard look. I always felt that anyone who was willing to stand on the end of a line like that just to see a picture, must be a right ass. But Maureen wanted to see the film and I stood with her for forty-five minutes and I didn't say one word against it. And I resented that, hating her for having that kind of power over me.

Once we were inside and she was holding my hand I loved her and I forgot that I was annoyed with myself for being such a spineless bastard. And a few times when I turned to whisper something to her and my lips brushed the side of her face this electric thing would happen again and nothing would be further from my mind than the film we'd queued to up see. And I stopped fighting it. When I was with Maureen I didn't care about anything or anybody else, not Guinness or Redmond or Larry or even Ma.

Yet when I was in the pub with Redmond I hardly thought about her, and once or twice, to help Harry out, I made up a foursome when he had a couple of softies lined up. It was odd, as if I had a split personality or something, because I enjoyed those times with Redmond, and there was just no getting away from it I loved a gargle and a bit of stray.

I'd been out steady with Maureen for three months before I tried to get into her. Not that I didn't want to, it was just that I was afraid of offending her and even losing her. Also I was putting quite a bit down with Mrs. Kearney, which helped me to control myself, even though Maureen was very hot stuff when you got her going.

One Friday night in midsummer we got off a bus at the top of Orwell Road, and without a word being said we were on our way down to the banks of the Dodder, Redmond's very own chlorophyll couch. It was a warm silent evening and there weren't a lot of people about for the time of year.

I was trembling as we walked down the stony hill that led to the river. It wasn't the weather and it wasn't just passion or whatever you call it; it was like a fear of what might happen, and the lack of conversation between us made it even worse.

At the bottom of the hill the ground changed under our feet. Tar and stones gave way to the earth path that cut through the river bank and the water moved beside us and we walked and I hoped that nobody would ever concrete or tarmac that path.

Lying together on the grass, the darkness slipping down like smoke, I kissed her mouth, and from the way she came back at me I knew she wanted me too. Kissing was no longer just kissing for its own sake, it was the build-up to having it off. There was no kidding about it, no trying to rub between her thighs with the back of the hand while you opened the fly buttons with the fingers at the same time. It was straightforward and honest and it was clean and beautiful. And afterwards I was afraid to move, afraid to smash this thing of being so close to her. And she held my face in her hands and she kept kissing my face and her lips were like velvet against my skin and I loved her more than all the world.

Yet somehow things had changed between us, something that I wasn't quite sure of. It was just that with Mrs. Kearney I wanted a good ride and so did she. With Maureen I wanted it too, but for some stupid reason I wanted her to stop me at the last moment. It was as if the way I felt about her depended on her purity, and the feeling was so strong that I must have gotten it across to her, although I didn't open my mouth.

'You're upset?'

I pushed my face into her neck and hair. Even in the dark I couldn't lie to her and look at her at the same time.

'No, I'm okay, honest, I am.'

I loved her but I felt like crying. How did she know exactly what to do? I trembled and at the same time she read my mind.

'That wasn't the first time, Padd.' Her voice was like a little cool breeze and I knew that she was talking about herself and not about me.

'That doesn't matter.' I don't know how I pushed the words

beyond my lips. 'I love you, that's all I care about. Do you love me?'

She laughed happily, tightening her grip on me. 'Of course I do, silly. Would I be doing this with you if I didn't?'

I kissed her viciously in answer. I couldn't have spoken. If she had to be in love to do it and she'd done it before, then she'd loved someone else before me. I felt as if my heart had been kicked around a field.

'I'm older than you are, Padd. I loved another boy before I even knew you. It was over and done with ages ago. Don't let it come between us, it just isn't important.'

'I already told you, didn't I, it doesn't matter, it's none of my business.'

She kissed me on the mouth, her teeth biting into my lips and I tried to crush her beneath me on the grass. No matter what, I needed that Maureen. But I was hurt, bruised at the thought of her and somebody else, and when we made love again I made her cry out with the force of my movement and I despised myself for being such a child.

When it was over we lay there and the grass seemed long and very cold. I didn't ever want to get up and go. She'd given herself with everything she'd had and with the way I felt about her I was afraid to break it. Nothing could ever be that good again.

Walking up the hill to the main road I could feel the change between us. Even the touch of her hand seemed different. It was a kind of knowing touch, a secret thing of ours. It scared me a bit. I felt like a fella who'd spent all his money on a house and found out that the roof was useless. Her touch was like a responsibility on my skinny shoulders. And when we stopped under the tree by the bus stop she turned and kissed me and I knew I was right.

The whole thing had changed. She was all passionate now and if I'd wanted to I could have given her an upright there on the street. That's how bad it was. Her tongue was like a whip-lash in and out of my mouth, and though I loved it it made me kind of sad. All our kisses in future would be like that, the lead-in to the ride. It was as if innocence had died, dried right up in those few hours on the Dodder.

I tried not to think about it. Stop being dramatic, Maguire, I kept on saying to myself as we kissed. Then she took my hand and put it up under her skirt on the soft part of her thighs above her stockings, and it was done so casually that I almost cried out. The same thing couldn't have happened two hours before and my eyelids nearly melted into each other with the pressure that I used to keep the tears back. It wasn't everyone who would understand a fella crying over a thing like that. It's funny, really, how the illusion of what something would be like, if you could do it, is so much better than the thing itself, when you do manage it. I can tell you I was glad when the bus came along.

We were quiet on the walk up Leinster Road, but I wasn't happy about the way she was holding my arm. And I was bloody glad to be off the bus. I'd had to chat her all the way down to Rathmines to stop her making an exhibition of both of us. She was rearing to go again and mad as I felt I was I drew the line at having it off on the top deck of a bus.

It was as if she owned my arm and that was a feeling that worried me, even though a few months before I would have given anything for her to hold on to me like that. We were passing the garage doorway where I'd first kissed her and there was a soldier and a mot wrapped around each other. With him being in the Army it was a dot on the card that the mot was a domestic of some kind, and as we passed she said to him, 'Kiss me, darlin', kiss me again,' in a voice that was straight from the arsehole of Kerry. And you could tell she was trying to do a take-off of the mot in the film at The Stella, and thinking of all the times that I used a bit of George Raft or someone else like that I burst out laughing. And I grabbed Maureen's hand and we ran together up the lane and I laughed so much that she couldn't help but join in and even when we stopped I felt relieved. She'd let go of my arm.

It's a funny thing about the soldiers of the Irish Republic. They get most of the country girls that come to Dublin to work as domestic servants. And it can't be the uniform, rough green material with about as much cut to it as a lamp post, a small boat-shaped hat on the side of the head, or a badly designed peaked cap, blood-red boots with short leggings that give the wearer a deformed look. That uniform was enough to make a Dublin fella look like he came from the bogs, so you can imagine what if did for the fellas who came from Kerry and Cork and 'The Wesht'.

Still, there was no doubt about it, the country girls liked the boys in uniform. The wearin' of the green did more for those fellas than it ever did for the patriots and the fanatics who shot each other to pieces to the air of Napper Tandy. And the local whoremasters were very put out about the whole thing.

Those girls who came to work in Dublin were one of the main sources of sexual pleasure to the ramrods of Rathmines and Rathgar, but the fact that the soldiers snaffled up most of it before it got its bags off the train meant that the demand was greater than the supply. And, of course, there were a certain number of the mots didn't want to know anyway, which made things even worse.

The locals would stand around in groups slagging the lucky green uniforms as they passed with a big pair of hips in a coloured frock beside them, and the endless chat that went on didn't produce any real reason as to why the girls preferred soldiers. It might have been because so many of the fellas in uniform were country people, but I think it was more than that.

The soldiers were willing to take the girls out and to be seen walking with them. The locals just wanted a quick jump or whatever else was going and good night, not caring in the least that the girls had feelings and wanted to be treated decently. And that poor cow in the doorway with her 'Kiss me, darlin',' head on her wasn't anything to laugh at, but really I was laughing because I thought it funny that she was doing the sort of thing that I did all the time.

I kissed Maureen good night again by the gate. I'd already agreed to go up to the house the next night. Her parents were going to be out, and now that we'd started on the full shilling I agreed with her that we might as well go to bed and do it in comfort whenever we got the chance.

By the time I got back to Rathmines Road I'd gotten over the worry of her feeling that she owned me. Nobody owned me and nobody ever would. I could sling Maureen or any other mot out any time I felt like it. I went out with her because I fancied her double strong and the minute I found that I was cheesed off with her I'd put an end to it. And that was all there was to it. After telling myself all this for a good few minutes I realised that I was trying to convince myself of something.

Yet again at the end of the lane I felt the flats reach out and touch me. I stopped the bike and walked back to the corner. I looked up along Mount Pleasant Avenue, raising my eyes in the darkness to where I knew the Dublin mountains sat looking down at me. I wondered if they knew I was feeling sorry for myself or if they realised how much I hated living on The Hill, or how much I cursed and swore, hating everybody who'd been lucky enough to be born on Palmerston Road or somewhere just as nice. But then the mountains couldn't have understood. I didn't myself.

Ma was awake when I got in. I didn't put on the light, but I knew by her breathing that she'd been waiting until she heard my key in the lock. And if I put on the light she'd start talking. Just then I didn't feel like talking to anyone. I headed as quietly as I could towards the bedroom door.

'Yer late, son.' Her voice was barely above a whisper, but it cut through me like a knife.

'Sorry to wake you, Ma. I tried not to.'

'You didn't wake me. I wasn't asleep. Where were you till now?'

'Ah, I was just out.' I knew it sounded weak, but it was the best I could do.

'Well, there's no good on the streets at this hour. You shouldn't be so late.'

I was still standing by the bedroom door. 'Okay. I'm sorry, Ma. 'Night.'

There was no having a go at Ma or telling her to mind her own business. When she pulled me up like that it was for my own good and I took it the way it was meant.

'Good night, son. God bless you.'

God bless you, the all-time stand by of the Irish mother. They held on to God and His Blessed Mother and all the others like a drowning man would hold on to a plank of wood. They didn't do it consciously. They believed in God and they loved him, but they didn't see that they were clinging on to him because they just didn't have anything else to hold on to. Their grey sad hearts got more than a fair share of rain but sunshine was as scarce as fillet steak.

As I took off my shoes Billy was lying on his back and he was cutting up timber like a bloody sawmill. I wished I'd had the guts to have a leak down his throat. That would shut up his snoring, and what a yarn it would have been to tell Harry Redmond. I moved as quickly as I could. If I woke him up there'd be a fist fight and with the way I was feeling he could have broken me up in little bits. I got into bed in my shirt. I didn't like wearing it to sleep in because of trying to keep it clean for the office, but if I got in in the nude the blankets made my skin itch, so the shirt was on twenty-four-hour call.

I woke up in an awful sweat after the worst nightmare I ever had in my life. It was so bad that I was glad to wake up and find I was at home on The Hill. Even that was heaven compared to the nightmare.

I was in short trousers and I was walking down the aisle to marry Maureen. Nobody seemed to care about the sight of my knees, but I was very nervous, and as I got near the old Canon, who was a right crotchety old bastard, he gave me a bull's look. And his voice as he read the marriage bit was like hot razor blades tearing around the inside of my head. Instead of his usual monotonous bleat he was punching it out like a bloody machine gun and he was putting the fear of Christ right up me.

I didn't look at Maureen but I knew she'd be looking okay. She wasn't all that big for four months. Her oul' fella was behind us and he was built like a brick shithouse. I could feel his eyes boring holes in the back of my head and that was something that I could have lived without.

Just then I was asked if I'd take Maureen to be my this, that and the other. For one second I didn't answer. I couldn't. Then I took a deep breath and I yelled into the old Canon's face, 'I will in my ballocks', and I turned and ran out of the church.

I was spewing my guts up into a geranium bed in one corner of the churchyard when her two brothers started filling me in. They slung punches in from every angle and I was so sick that I couldn't even put my hands up. When I fell down they put the boot into me and I started to black out from a kick in the head. But just before I went out cold I saw my blue-eyed Maureen getting into this big black car that was like a hearse and I could have sworn she gave me a wink with the left eye.

Was it any wonder I woke up in a sweat? God, it had been so real that I felt my face in the dark for a minute before I was sure that the nose hadn't been kicked right off me. And as I said, it was good to be in my own bed, even if it was on The Hill. I listened for a few seconds, wondering if I'd woken Ma. Josie and Billy I wasn't worried about, but Ma needed her sleep.

How would she feel when I finally left the place? How would it affect her when I was no longer there with a cheeky word or a few bob when she needed it? That was the hard part, hard for both of us. Ma was the one person I'd never had a mean thought about in my life. She was the one light in that dark miserable hole. She added dignity to the word mother.

All her life Ma followed her heart, the head coming a very poor second. Even when she met the oul' fella it was the same thing. She loved him and she went to the altar with him. It wasn't a practical thing to do but she didn't care who he was or where he came from. And years later, when she found out that love on its own just isn't enough, when poverty and all that poverty breeds showed her that much, she didn't blame anybody. She got on with the job of trying to feed and dress her kids. enduring the awful, hopeless, endless business, giving them all she could and crying only over the things that she wasn't able to provide. Love didn't die, it just got pushed aside. There wasn't time for love in the pit of her existence. Yet love was all she had, all she could afford to have, and this only gave her more children until in the end the one thing that she needed to keep her going was slowly but surely choking her to death. So God, sweet, lovely, impotent God, was loved, and man slept alone.

I did drift off to sleep again but I felt rough in the morning. I was sticky and uncomfortable between the legs. Maureen was all over my stomach and I wouldn't have washed her off except that I felt dirty. The cold water soon knocked the sleep out of my eyes and I hated it. I've no time for this good health chat about a cold wash, winter and summer. Give me hot water every time.

Maureen filled my thoughts all through the paper round and I felt warm just for thinking about her. Apart from loving her and wanting her I liked her. She was a cheeky little cow and it was great fun to be with her and even in that bloody awful nightmare she'd been on my side, even though I had left her standing at the altar. I smiled when I thought about that. If I'd gone as far as the church, even if it was a shotgun wedding, I wouldn't have had the guts to do what I did in the dream. I wasn't that much a man and I didn't think I ever would be. There aren't too many people about who can be that true to themselves. So, I would just have to make sure it never got to that stage unless I wanted to end up married with a load of kids.

By half past ten Cahill was stuck into me in front of the whole general office. God, I don't know how I kept my knuckles out of his mouth. I wouldn't have minded if he'd had something to moan about, but it was so stupid that you could tell he was taking it out on me because he'd had a row with his missus or something. Probably wanted a slice off the legs before his porridge, and when he hadn't got it he'd come in to take it out on someone. And who could be easier than Maguire.

'Here, Maguire,' he called, with the slow snide smile on his rubber mouth for the benefit of his typist who was taking shorthand at his desk. 'Would you be kind enough to translate this for me? I can only read English.'

I took the copy proposal form from his hand, thinking that if his shitty nature could have showed his face would have been Technicolor.

'Sorry, Mr. Cahill, which part is it?' The words were like lumps of clay as they came out of my mouth.

Up came his head from the thing he was pretending to read and his face like a bucket of vomit. 'It's the whole thing, Maguire. What do you write with, a snail?'

He made sure that the whole office could hear him. His eyes flicked from me to the typist—was she smiling at his repartee? I looked hard at the form and I honestly couldn't see anything wrong with it. I read out the make and date of the car, its value, the fact that the proposer had agreed to carry a voluntary five-pound accidental-damage excess and that he was entitled to a second-year no-claim bonus. He took the form back with a big show of impatience and he wrote over my writing. I didn't move. I could feel that there was more to come.

'I hope we're not going to go through this every time you copy a proposal form. You'll have to pay more attention to what you're doing.'

'Yes, sir,' I said, and I walked back to my desk, my face as red as a bottle of blood.

I sat there for a minute, trying to find the guts to walk back up to the bastard and spit in his face. I was kidding myself, I knew that, but I wanted to hurt that man if it was the last thing I ever did.

Larry Deegan walked up the office just then, and as he passed me he gave me a wink and I knew from the way he did it that he was going to talk to Cahill. It was that certain look he wore when he had something up his sleeve, and I sat and listened.

'That premium for O'Day's fleet.'

'What about it?' Cahill asked.

'It's out by forty-two pounds,' Larry said loudly, but he was so matter-of-fact that he might have been asking the time.

'It can't be,' Cahill said, with a little laugh as if he'd sat on the nib of a pen. 'It can't be, Deegan. I worked it out myself.'

'You forgot the ten per cent load.' Larry wasn't arguing. He was telling him.

There wasn't a sound as Cahill looked at the calculation. He made hard work of it, sucking at his teeth, then the deep sigh as if he were dying. 'Oh, yes, I see. Yes, that does make a difference, doesn't it?'

He laughed again, acting confident, but he didn't fool anyone in the office. They knew him too well for that.

'Ah, well, it's good to know you're not infallible.'

He tried to make it sound as though he were talking about Larry. And that was it, no apology, no word of thanks, nothing.

Larry walked back down to his desk and I felt like jumping up and clapping him on the back. As far as I was concerned people could do that to Cahill all day. There wasn't one thing about that man that I could take. For me, he took the good out of everything. If he felt like saying good morning, he did, but most times he just didn't bother. And if you said it first he was likely to say 'Is it?', as if the joke was original. He just didn't have a bit of class, that man, and most people, no matter who they are or where they come from, have a little bit, even if it's only a very little bit.

Being a Saturday, it was early closing and I was glad of that. I felt really tired after the nightmare and I had a pain in my back from the carry on with Maureen on the river bank. And I'd had a phone call from Mrs. Kearney. I hadn't been up to see her all week, so I promised to call on Sunday afternoon. I told her that I'd been studying for an insurance examination, and whether she believed me or not she was happy enough when I said I'd be up the next day. She was all right and it was decent of her to give me that dollar a week. Every little bit helped.

Larry and I went for a drink after work and it was a gift to get on the outside of a few bottles of stout. The little boozer that we used was clean and the atmosphere was friendly and it was handy for both of us. And the Guinness there was so good that I didn't envy Larry as he knocked back whiskey on the rocks, as though it was pure gold.

He was a great pal to me, that Larry, and even then I knew that I'd never be able to pay him back for the confidence he'd given me. And it wasn't just when I'd had a few drinks that I felt that way. We often sat over a coffee and talked and I never failed to learn something from him. He proved to me that worry was a sort of negative thing, that in itself it solved nothing. Through him I learned to shrug at things that would have really bothered me only a short time before. He showed me that you had to take life as it came, the way he did himself.

Ma had been a worrier all her life and all she got out of it was a head of grey hair. The oul' fella too, I now realised, had made himself into a grumpy impossible man because he was worried all the time about finding work. It's funny, and yet at the same time very sad, but he worried about his wife and kids to such a pitch that he became unbearable, and the wife and the kids that were the cause of it all just stopped loving him.

It wasn't the fault of any of them. The situation was there and the people involved in it had no choice. Somehow they had been dropped into place by a careless hand, left sitting up to their necks in poverty and pain and misery without ever knowing why.

10

MYSELF and Larry were still in the pub at ten minutes to closing time, and he was standing up to order the last round when this girl gave him a push in the back. He turned round and he lit up when he saw who it was.

'Breeda. Ah hello, good to see you.'

She was a tall dark-haired girl with a heavy well-shaped body and when she smiled I could see that her teeth were good. Her hair was cropped very short, which was good on her because her eyebrows were firm over warm dark eyes. Her mouth was large with soft fleshy lips and I thought she was really something. She wore a blue costume that somehow seemed almost casual on her and the straight seams of her stockings were a gift to look at.

'Knocking them back, are you?'

'Boredom,' he said, winking an eye at me. 'I was just now saying to Paddy here that Breeda was needed to give this place a boost.'

She watched him closely as he spoke and I could see that she was fond of him.

'This is Breeda Connell, Paddy. Breeda, meet a very good friend of mine, Paddy Maguire.'

I stood up and we shook hands and I liked the firm grip that she gave me.

'Watch out for this fella Paddy, he's fly.'

She smiled when she said it and you couldn't help liking her.

'Pleased to meet you, Breeda,' I said, and really meant it.

She let go of my hand and I stopped looking at her. I didn't know what the score was between Larry and herself and I didn't want to offend him.

'Watch out for yourself with him, Breeda,' Larry said as he put a drink in front of her on the table, 'he's a tiger with the women.'

'But he looks so young,' she said, and even a remark like that was okay from her.

'Well, why shouldn't he?' Larry said, 'he's only nineteen.'

I was beginning to know Larry's form by now, so I managed not to look surprised. Breeda was still looking at me and she didn't seem to doubt for a minute that Larry was telling the truth. That gave me a boost. That twice-weekly shave that I didn't really need must have been bringing a bit of stubble out at last.

Larry was buying more drink and Breeda sat down on the bench seat beside me.

'Are you in insurance, Paddy?'

'Yeh. The same office as Larry. He's a great fella.'

'I'm glad you think so,' she smiled wickedly. 'He drinks too much.'

'Sure, nobody's perfect,' I said, the Guinness gone to my head by this time.

Instantly she was sad, almost in tears. Then a quick, weary sort of smile and she seemed all right again.

'Sorry, Breeda, did I say something to offend you?'

I tried to remember what it was I had said, but I was feeling the drink now and I just couldn't make it. But I had the odd feeling that I'd been the cause of her sudden and brief sadness.

'No, Paddy, I'm sorry. It's just me. I get a bit miserable some-times. I'm a funny old stick.'

Larry came back with more drinks so we didn't get any further with that conversation. He'd bought two bottles of stout for me and I knew that when I drank those I'd be well and truly cut.

I didn't argue with him about it or about all the drinks he'd been buying all afternoon. It was useless to bother. He'd only repeat that money was made round to go round.

When we left the pub I wanted to shoot off and leave him with Breeda, but he wouldn't hear of it. I was drunk enough not to be able to ride the bike, but that wouldn't have stopped me. Larry just wouldn't let me go and even Breeda, who didn't seem all that keen for me to go with them, began to press me when she saw that Larry was in earnest.

I stood with her while he hailed a taxi and after he had a chat with the driver my bike was slung across the boot of the car. Then we were all together on the back seat, singing our way to Merrion Square where, by all accounts, Breeda had a flat.

It was one of those Georgian houses that everybody raves about, except Dubliners themselves. The particular house that Breeda lived in was in a bit of a state. All dirty and tired-looking, and worn, like an old boot. You could see that it would take more than a few pots of paint to put it right, but I didn't care. Houses like that were, to me, relics of another time that was best forgotten. The good old days when privilege was the clobber worn only by the upper classes. My two grannies had scrubbed the steps of houses like that and they'd never entered them except by the tradesmen's entrance, as the side door was called. Kind words and gestures of appreciation had been scarce. The gentry had but little to say to pot-washers and step-scrubbers. So, drunk as I was, I looked at it and felt nothing that it was falling to bits. I had no tears for houses like that.

The taxi driver was asked in for a drink, and more power to his elbow he didn't say no. Dublin taximen are like that. If the work interferes with the drinking, stop the work. He was a nice friendly oul' fella with plenty of Blarney, and the colour of his nose had cost him more than the value of his taxi, if looks were anything to go by.

Breeda's flat looked comfortable and Larry flopped down on

the settee in the big lounge, as though he owned the place. And I thought to myself, Jeysus, maybe he does! Nothing about that fella could have surprised me.

Breeda got some tumblers and poured drinks all round. The taxi driver gave his whiskey an awful quick death. She gave him another and that didn't live long either, then he was shaking hands with us and he was gone. Talk about a quick drink.

I sat down and felt really drunk. Breeda put on a record and herself and Larry started to dance. They seemed to be stuck together at the crotch and they didn't move more than the length of a hankie. It wasn't really what you could call dancing, it was more like a dry upright. I enjoyed watching them shuffle about and they were still at it when I fell off to sleep.

They weren't in the room when I woke up. I could see from the mantle clock that I'd been asleep for about an hour and I felt that I was going to be sick. I went to the door hoping to find a bathroom and my head felt like a ton of turf. When I got into the hall I could hear a bed going like the clappers. For once I wasn't interested in sex and I only just got to the lavatory pan in time. God, was I sick! I swear it came up from the soles of my feet and there was a stone-cold sweat on my face by the time I finished. I had a good wash, first with hot and after with cold water. Then I took some toothpaste from a tube on the wash-basin and rubbed it into my mouth and teeth. After a good gargle I felt a lot better. Then I went back into the lounge and there was Larry putting another record on the gramophone. He seemed relieved that I looked okay.

'All right?'

'Yeh. Sorry. Hope I didn't spoil things for you.'

He shook his head. 'No, I'd had my share when I heard you being sick. Fancy a drink?'

'No, not right now, thanks.' God, I didn't ever want to get near a drink again, as long as I lived.

Guy Mitchell came off the record, singing about his truly

truly fair and it was okay to listen to. I sat down and Larry sipped from his glass.

'Breeda likes you. It's there if you fancy it.'

I fancied her all right. I thought she had everything that a woman should have. But going in after him seemed a bit strong. I honestly felt that he wouldn't care one way or the other but I didn't want him, above all people, to think I was a jibber.

'It won't be easy following you,' I grinned, 'but I'll do the best I can.'

He laughed and swallowed the rest of his drink. 'Good on you. You're a man after me own heart.'

I left him standing there and went along the hall to the room where she lay in the bed. I closed the door after me and she opened her eyes. She looked as though she was only half in the room. Her dark eyes were glazed and her mouth looked raw from where I stood. She sat up and the sheet fell away from her breasts. They stood out firm, the nipples like brown eyes against the cream of her skin. My throat was dry and I was so tense that I thought my skin would crack. I didn't move. I couldn't.

'You've come to make love to me, Paddy.' Her voice was dry as parchment. 'Come in with me in the bed.'

I took my clothes off without thinking about what I was doing. It was automatic, no thought about it, just an action that was to lead to something else.

I stood by the bed and she reached out and took my hands. I fell down beside her and she kissed me, taking me with her into a pink and green confusion of love-making. It was fierce and even painful and I remember that she begged to be bitten and even her blood on my lips seemed all right.

When I got out of bed Larry got back in beside her and I went into the bathroom and lay soaking in glorious hot water. My body stung all over and when I looked at myself I saw that I was a mass of bruises. I lay there in sweet luxury, feeling that this was the life.

About six o'clock we went into the local pub and I was surprised to find that I wanted a bottle of Guinness, when only a few hours before I was swearing to myself that I'd never touch a drink again.

We talked and joked over the drinks, but the happenings of the afternoon weren't mentioned. Larry was his usual happy-go-lucky self and Breeda was just as she'd been when I first met her, except for little dark shadows that were under her eyes. I tried not to keep looking at her, but it wasn't easy. I'd never known anyone quite like her and I wanted more of the same.

When I got up to go she kissed me full on the mouth and I knew that she liked me. Either that or she was some actress.

'Goodbye, Breeda. See you soon.'

'Sure,' she said. 'Nice to meet you, Paddy.'

For some reason I didn't expect her to be any different to the way she was just then. I didn't expect any thanks, any more than she did from me. I can't explain it, it was just the way she affected me. What we'd had in the afternoon was over and done with. It had nothing to do with us saying goodbye.

Larry came out to the bike with me and, though I tried arguing, he shoved a ten-bob note in the top pocket of my jacket.

'Don't be such a worrier, it's made round to go round.'

I knew he'd say that, but there was no point in telling him that a ten-bob note was oblong. He'd have told me to change it into four half-crowns and see how round they were, or something like that. Neither of us said anything about Breeda. I just said so long to him and I rode off towards home, half afraid that I'd wake up and find that I'd been dreaming.

I gave Ma half a dollar when I got in and told her that I'd been washing the boss's car, which was why I was late. She seemed to believe me and gave me a boiled egg and some bread and butter for my tea.

It's a bloody awful thing to tell a lie to someone you love, and it seems even worse when they believe you. If they doubt you a little bit you don't feel so bad, and if they don't believe a word you say it's even better. You can argue with them in your mind and end up convincing yourself that if that's the way they are you did right to bullshit them in the first place. You can vindicate yourself to yourself, even though you know that you're nothing but a bloody liar.

When Billy came in I was in the scullery using his razor. He went wild with temper and he'd have beaten the bejeysus out of me if Ma hadn't come out of the kitchen and saved my bacon. She told me off for using his razor though.

'You've enough money to buy one of your own, if you must shave.'

'He's got nothing to shave,' Billy snorted. 'He's only a maneen, trying to be big.'

'You'll get my fist in your gob, Porky,' I yelled at him, knowing that Ma wouldn't let us fight.

'That's enough, Paddy. Stoppit.' Ma used a tone that meant just that and I shut up tight. It made me feel a bit better, her having a go at me like that. It sort of evened things up for me lying earlier about the boss's car. Billy gave me a look that should have melted me on the spot and he went straight out again, slamming the door so hard behind him that it nearly followed him out on to the street.

On the way up to see Maureen I stopped in at the pub for a few bottles of stout. I thought I'd have a few. If she expected the same kind of performance that we'd had last night up on The Dodder I'd need something to give me strength.

Redmond was there as usual and I bought a couple of rounds. Then he got up to buy one and he got a bit snotty at the look of surprise on my face.

'Don't be so bleedin' smart,' he rasped at me out of his crooked mouth. 'We're not all working in the insurance game, you know.'

'Ah, leave off, Harry, for Jeysus' sake. I never said a word.'

'You didn't have to, boy. A nod is as good as a wink to a blind man. When I have it I spend it.' He began to grin. 'The only trouble is I never shaggin' well have it.'

'Haven't seen you much recent,' he said, sitting down.

'I know, I've been reciting a bit of poetry.'

He looked at me, knowing full well what I meant. 'Ah, holy Jeysus, is nothing sacred any more?'

He drank some of the Guinness. 'Mind you, it's my own fault. I tell you how to do it, and before you can strain the potatoes every prick in Rathmines'll be using my approach.'

'Don't kid yourself,' I said. 'You don't think I'm going to put it around, do you? No fear, that line belongs to you and me.'

He drew breath so hard that he nearly swallowed the butt he was sucking. 'Jeysus, it's awful decent of you to put me in. Thanks a million.' He looked up at the ceiling, as though he was talking to someone else. 'Marvellous, isn't it, not out of short trousers a bleedin' week. Honest to Jeysus, I don't know what the world is coming to, I don't really.'

Redmond was well known around Rathmines and he was accepted as a great fella for taking a rise out of people. Now I had him going strong and he didn't even realise it. I took a mouthful of stout, swallowed it down and grinned at him. 'Still, I'm old enough to buy porter for you. Anyway, you needn't fret. I won't be poaching on your territory. I've only been with the one scivvie and that was only to help you out.'

'Golden ballocks,' he slammed the glass on the table, 'that's a good name for you.' He started talking to the ceiling again. 'Doesn't have to bother with domestic servants, if you don't mind.' He looked at me and his eyes were boiling. 'Listen, sunshine, right now, this very fuckin' minute, I could take you to a couple of mots that'd suck you in and blow you out in bleedin' bubbles.'

'Ah, but they're only oul' rough, Harry. Sure everyone's at them.'

'Will you shut your mouth and give your arse a chance.' He pushed the glass towards me. 'Buy a drink for the luvva God.'

I got up willingly to buy another round. I'd buy drink all night for the pleasure of getting Redmond going. When I sat down again I thought I'd go a bit stronger. I was thinking of Breeda asking me to bite her. She liked to be hurt, and though I didn't understand it I was excited by it, so I built it up before I said a word to Redmond.

'Have you ever beaten a mot with a cane, Harry?'

I asked him in the same way that I'd ordered a drink and he looked as if he was going to drop the glass.

'A cane?' He said it as he were being tortured. 'Is that what you're learnin' in the insurance office?'

I sipped the stout. 'Well, have you or haven't you?'

He didn't answer me. He didn't want to admit to something that I might think was odd. It took him a good few seconds to make up his mind. Then all he could do was ask me why.

'Ah, it's this mot I know. Loves being beaten with a cane, she does. Terrific-looking mot too.'

His eyes had a faraway look. 'Jeysus, a masochist! God's gift to man.'

'What's that?'

'A masochist? Someone who gets a thrill out of suffering. You know, the opposite to a sadist.' His voice was vague and crispy dry.

'Oh, yeah,' I said, 'I thought that's what it was.'

He was back with me now, the faraway look had gone out of his eyes. 'Where'd you come across her, then?'

'A party I went to the other night.'

'And you've beaten her, have you?' He was breathless at the very idea, and I wouldn't have gone on with it except that he was such a ruthless bastard when he had anybody else on the hook.

'Yeh, sure I have. You've got to give them what they want, haven't you?'

'That's the only snag with them bleedin' pot-wallopers,' he complained. 'They're ordinary, small-minded, you know. Oh, they'll do it all right, up to their eyes in muck, they'll do it. No bloody imagination, though, that's the trouble with them. You mention variation on a theme and they think it's a feckin' greyhound or something.'

'You've never had one, then?'

'Me?' He hesitated just for a fraction of a second and I knew he was going to start telling bloody lies. "Course I have. Married bird, she was. Well off, crazy about me, couldn't give her enough of it. Never knew an intellectual before, see. Rich eejits. That's all she'd ever had up her. Loved to be hurted she did, absolutely loved it.'

'In what way?'

'Ah, now, that'd be tellin', wouldn't it.'

I sat back and kept quiet. He was kidding and I knew it, but he didn't know I was kidding him. That gave me a real lift. You had to get up very early in the day to catch Harry Redmond. He had a big reputation around Rathmines, so I must have been coming on to have got him going like that. It was the start of the change in our relationship. He no longer dominated the chats we had. Even with Harry I was beginning to hold my own.

I stood up and emptied my glass. 'I'm off now, Harry. Don't want to keep her waiting too long.'

'Where's she live, then?'

'Ah now, that'd be telling, wouldn't it?' I grinned and went out of the snug. Then, instead of turning right for the street I went left up the passage and stood there. The door hadn't stopped swinging after me when he came through it and without so much as a glance in my direction he went out into the street. I started to whistle and walked down the passage to where he stood, just outside the door. He turned and his face dropped when he saw that it was me. 'Bloody stuffy in there,' he said.

'I'll have one for you before I get dressed,' I said. 'About twelve o'clock. Okay?'

He didn't say a word, but he stood there as I put on my cycle clips. He wanted to see which way I was heading. I took my time, messing about with the saddle and all the rest of it, and after a few minutes he went back inside. Then I jumped up on the bike and went up Leinster Road before he could get back out to have another look.

Maureen was in a dressing gown when she opened the door and I was hardly inside before she was in my arms. The ice had been broken between us and now it was all straightforward. I felt the heat of her and she was as soft as a mushroom and it was a rich feeling to lie beside her in the bed. I was feeling all the better for the drinks that I'd had with Harry, and to be loving Maureen and to have the feeling that she needed me there. God, it was something for a fella to relish in his old age!

It seemed so natural to be there in the bed with her, even though it was my first time in the house. I didn't stop for a second and wonder what would happen if her oul' fella came back and caught me. I should have done, I suppose, because by all accounts he was a real hard nut, the sort of an oul' fella who'd as soon kick you as shake you by the hand. A lot of oul' fellas were like that. They pulverised you first and asked what you were doing afterwards. It was a sobering thought, if you thought about it, which I didn't at the time. I mean, Maureen's da could have taken a skinny fella like me and pulled me into little pieces without so much as removing his jacket. Anyway, he didn't show up, so it was just as well I didn't ruin my evening by worrying.

Maureen seemed to find me a bit different than before. She was giving me a strange look every so often, and after the third time, as we lay into one another, she was acting as though I was Jesus Christ or someone. It was a great feeling, sort of like having power over her and I enjoyed it more than I should have done. It wasn't right to want to have influence over her. She was a very nice person and it was bad to want to pull strings and watch her jump. But that's exactly what I wanted.

Even worse, I was patting myself on the back for being such a smart fella, as if I was responsible for the way I was shaping. I didn't realise that my ability to take all kinds of situations in my stride was just pure luck. Luck at running into the right people at the right time, luck at being born in the flats. Yes, The Hill, the place I hated most on earth. The place where you learned early whether you wanted to or not. The tough, dirty, cage, where you had to hit and bite and snarl harder and more viciously than the other fella, if you ever wanted anything other than kicks or bumps for the rest of your life. Just being born there gave you a head start on most people. Rarely did you get a second chance, so the first time you learned something it stuck. It had to stick.

So if I was good at soaking things up it had very little to do with me being the clever cock I thought I was. And if I could bend with the breeze or bounce back from a body blow it was because of where I'd been born and because of the way that I'd had to grow up. It was all part of being part of The Hill.

11

THE mad Saturday afternoon with Larry and Breeda and the evening in bed with Maureen had really knocked me out, so that when I was on the bus on my way to see Mrs. Kearney it was only the thought of the dollar that kept me going.

I was tired and weary and if it hadn't been for the Guinness that I'd had at lunchtime I'd have fallen asleep where I sat. The Sunday queue was outside The Stella, but I didn't mind that I wasn't going to be there. I didn't feel that I had the energy to chat up a mot, let alone wrestle with her in the seat for the afternoon. I was starting to realise that even though sex was the greatest, too much of it was likely to leave you feeling as though your spine, or your backbone, or whatever it is that keeps your back straight, had been taken away.

I opened the window beside my head and a cool flow of sunshine breeze came through. It was a lovely day, what you might call good-to-be-alive weather, and I enjoyed seeing the soldiers and their mots stepping it out towards the Dodder. A lot of the girls had big legs and good hips, and in their coloured dresses they looked more than all right.

I wondered if they were as good as Redmond claimed. I couldn't tell. The one I'd walked with that night to help him out had been so innocent that I didn't have the heart to try and give her one. Honestly, I felt such a bastard that night, telling her endless lies and getting her going an' all, that in the finish I'd just had a good necking session and tried to convince her that all fellas weren't pigs. I don't know why I did it. I guess she just touched something in me that I didn't even know was there. And I was so nice to her, not that I meant a word of it, that I think she'd fallen for me by the time I left her. It wasn't a bad thing to do, I suppose, but it didn't help me to be any judge about scivvies.

Big hips made me think of Breeda, and I knew that with or without Larry I was going to try and see her again. Larry was the greatest and God knows he'd been more than good to me, but I couldn't help the way I felt. I had to see her again if I got even half a chance. I suppose it was thinking about Breeda that gave me a hard on, that and the sun shining in on me in the bus. I sat there thinking what a bloody nuisance it was. I didn't have a coat or a newspaper or anything to hold in front of me as I got off. And you feel such a bloody fool and the more you try and think of something else, so that'll it die, the harder it gets. And I feel sure that some of them scrubbers that know more than they should about men look for it when you get up off the seat. You walk along the aisle and when you glance at them they're not looking at your face, as you might expect, they're blimping your crotch to see if you're bulging a bit. No respect for a fella's privacy.

Breeda's age had a lot to do with the way she attracted me, I knew that. Twenty-nine or so, she was, and it seemed a great thing to me that I could possibly interest a woman of that age, especially such an attractive one. She was really lovely with that big sensuous body and even the fact that she was some kind of masochist didn't frighten me off. And I knew that if she'd have asked me to go and live with her or go away to England with her, or anything like that, she wouldn't have got no for an answer. Not Maureen or Ma, not anything could have stopped me.

It wasn't a bright way to be thinking, I knew that. Just one afternoon, sharing her with Larry at that. When you thought about it it wasn't much of a reference for a mot and yet it didn't matter a damn to me. With Maureen I'd wanted her to be a virgin. I'd even needed for her to be one, but with Breeda I didn't care. No matter what she'd done or who'd been there before me I still wanted her, and I didn't even want to know about anything what had happened before we met. The way I felt about her was very different to my love for Maureen. It was a wild thing and odd and strange and ugly, but if I'd had to make a choice there was no doubt in my mind that it was Breeda I'd have run to.

I stopped looking at the girls on the street and I tried hard to stop thinking about sex, and for no reason at all I found that I was calling myself names. I felt like a louse so often that I must have begun to look like one, so I was a louse and a sort of shit-hot smart alec who knew it all. I didn't like myself very much just then, but I was the way I was and all the thinking about it and all the false promises in the world weren't going to change me. Not one little bit. You can't change what's in your blood any more than you can change the colour of it.

It was a ten-minute walk from the bus stop to Mrs. Kearney's house and I tried to read a book as I walked along. It's not an easy thing to do. If you concentrate more on the walking you miss what's on the page; if you really get stuck into the story you keep stopping before you walk into lamp-posts that aren't there. And if the book is good, that's no way to read it anyway.

The one I was working on was A. J. Cronin's *Keys of the Kingdom*. It was a great story. God, the priest was a marvellous man altogether. So full of humility and tolerance and so very different from the arrogant white-collar workers that I'd come across, most of the time, that I loved him from the beginning. I felt that there must be men like him somewhere, men who became priests because there was no other life for them. It was a good thing to feel that they weren't all demigods in dark suits.

I scribbled a lot into my exercise books about that man, he

was so real to me, and it was about people like him that I wanted to write. People who gave of themselves just because that was how they were. People who gave without ever expecting anything in return.

I wanted to use him to help me write. Just to think about him gave me a glow. To me he was such a great person that I was full of good feeling when he was in my thoughts and when I felt that way I wanted to write all the time. But, like so many other times, the feeling went down the drain all too quickly. Telling yourself that you're going to do this and that is very easy. You can do it anytime, whether you're walking, drinking or making love. It takes little effort, but developing a sense of application, forcing yourself to sit down and put words on paper, ignoring the Guinness that was there for the drinking and the mots that were so available, that was the rough bit. And that's what I was up against, although it wasn't hard for me to write. I had a facility for putting words on paper and I was in love with the idea of being a writer, but I didn't have the backbone to go without the things that stopped me writing. I'd get down to it one day, I told myself every day. Meantime, there was stout for the drinking and there were girls.

I put the book away and when Mrs. Kearney opened the door she looked lovely. She had a new pair of glasses on, shaped like cat's eyes, and a white linen blouse that made me forget how tired I'd been on the bus. A kiss then and the warmth of her body against me and I'd forgotten everything except the fact that I'd been doing the same thing with Maureen only twelve or fourteen hours earlier.

There was a couple of dozen bottles of Arthur J. in the house and we had a good drink and a few beef sandwiches. She didn't eat much but she was putting the black stuff away as quick as I was myself. Then she told me that her husband was dead. Ten days ago, she said, and though she was very quiet she was so matter-of-fact about it that you could tell she had known, like

Ma with little Larry, that the tuberculosis would win in the end.

I felt very odd when she told me. There I was sitting eating the fella's roast beef and him getting colder with every bite I was taking. I told her that I was very sorry and I took another drink. It wasn't true. You can't be sorry someone's dead when you've never met the man. But I had to say something, lip service. You don't mean it and the people that you say it to know that you don't, but they're grateful that you took the trouble to say it. Courtesy, it's called, but I think bullshit would be a better name for it. There's so much of that kind of toffee in the world that you don't know what to believe any more.

'It was God's holy will,' she said, and she got up off the sofa and walked to the window.

'It's good to know that he's in heaven,' I said, looking at the shape of her hips in the black skirt and wishing to Christ that she'd change the subject.

It was the Clark Gable voice again, and I put so much feeling into it that she was close to tears when she turned round. It was a liberty to talk to her like that. I mean, I had no more idea of where her man was than I had of how to pull rabbits out of a hat. But I felt she'd want to hear something like that, so I just said it.

She came and sat beside me again and she touched my hand. 'You're very grown up, Paddy. It's hard to credit that you could be so sensitive.'

Jeysus, you're not kidding! I thought, and then I felt guilty for being such a smug little bastard.

'Did you have enough to eat?'

'Oh, yeh, it was great. Thanks a lot.'

She smiled a little and then she gave a big sigh as though she was very tired her breasts moved up and down under her blouse and I wanted to lean over and give them a good bite. They were so lovely that she must have known it. Honestly, they stood up like soldiers and you couldn't help feeling that they'd been made for better things than just having kids suck milk out of them.

'I've sold the house and the business, Paddy. I'm going home to Wicklow.'

I didn't know what to say to that. I had an awful feeling that my dollar a week was gone west. 'Are you further down than Bray?'

'Yes, down beyond Newtownmountkennedy. It's peaceful there and really lovely. I've never really settled in Dublin.'

There was something about the way she was saying all this. I couldn't put a finger on it. There was just something in her voice.

'I wish you could come with me, Paddy,' she said, and I knew then what had been puzzling me. It had been in her voice even before she said it. She leaned over and kissed me and I could tell, dead husband or no dead husband, she was dying for it. She held on to me and I was glad to be able to comfort her. I only hoped that her husband couldn't see what was going on. I mean it was his sofa and his missus.

Afterwards we went up to the bedroom and we lay together between white linen sheets and it was great. She talked about Wicklow as though she was trying to get me to buy the whole county. It sounded like a marvellous place and the idea of going down there to live was very attractive to me. I wouldn't have to work and I'd be able to get down to that book I'd been dreaming about. That was good to think about and she had enough money to make it possible. There wouldn't be any shortage of food or drink, and living under the same roof with her I'd get enough of the other to keep even me quiet.

I was kidding myself and I knew it. I hadn't a chance of getting away with it. If Ma ever found out that I was poncing on a woman nearly twice my age she'd curl up with shame and die. And anyway, I didn't think I'd be able to stick Mrs. Kearney for more than a week. She was okay and she was kind but I

124

didn't love her. At the same time I knew that if Breeda had made me the same offer I'd have gone with her like a shot, even at the risk of destroying Ma.

When I'd had a bath I looked at myself full length in the mirror and I was about as well built as a sixpenny candle. I couldn't imagine what Mrs. Kearney saw in me. Even when I posed and tried to look romantic I was still a skinny string of nothing. I shook my head at myself in the mirror. I'd have to do a Charles Atlas course or something. I couldn't go on as I was or I'd slip down a bloody drain.

When I was leaving she started to cry and it got on my nerves so much that I felt like hitting her. I just don't know how to cope with women crying. She held on to me and I kissed her, promising to go down to see her in Wicklow just as soon as I could. As I opened the door she put two pound notes into my hand and somehow I managed not to shout for joy. It was no time to look happy and she so upset, so I hugged her to me and she wept into my skinny shoulder and I didn't mind at all. And I thought to myself that I was getting really good at being a louse.

She promised to ring me at the office during the week and I kissed her then for the last time and I walked down the path and out along the road. When I got to the corner I turned and she was standing by the gate. I waved to her and she put her hand up to her mouth. Then I was round the corner and running and jumping along the footpath. And I'll tell you one thing, those two greenbacks were burning a hole in my pocket.

That night in the pub I flashed a ten-bob note under Redmond's nose. He looked at it with green eyes and when I told him that the mot with the cane had given it to me he was double-choked. He didn't want to believe it but he knew that I didn't earn enough to be carrying that kind of dough on a Sunday night. I bought the Guinness and we talked and I built everything up so much that he was livid with jealousy before I was half finished.

I didn't do it to hurt him, it was just practice. To be able to tell barefaced lies and not blink an eye was an art, and I wanted to be as good at it as Redmond was.

We drank a lot of stout and by about half nine I felt fine. Redmond was keen to go to the Mansion House. So much so that I felt he'd made a date to see the widow there, but when I stood up I knew I was too tired to go. Even after all the drink my legs were aching and for once in my life I decided to use a bit of common sense and go home to bed. Harry wasn't too pleased at me. If I didn't go that meant he couldn't either. He hadn't any money, so he was depending on me to carry him. He tried to talk me into it, but I was too tired even to listen. And he wouldn't ask me for the money to go on his own. Redmond would ask you for drink with no qualms whatsoever. It was said of him around Rathmines that he'd drink porter out of a whore's boot, but he wouldn't tap you for cash and I wasn't offering it, knowing that I would never get it back. So he walked around to the flats with me and though I thought the touch was sure to come he didn't ask me for a penny. Even Redmond had his pride.

Next morning in the office I gave Larry Deegan a twenty packet of fags, and he looked so much at a loss that I wished I hadn't done it. It was as if he'd never been given a present before in his life. 'Ah, you shouldn't have done that, kid.'

I walked down the office not knowing what to say. Later he whispered that he'd meet me for a coffee if I could get away for long enough and I said I'd see him in Grafton Street. That was far enough away from the office for us not to be seen and at the same time handy enough for both of us.

I arrived there about half ten and he was waiting for me in a horsebox seat. The smell of the freshly roasted coffee was like a drug to me and I sat down filling my lungs with it. I liked the place so much that I'd have gone there every morning if I'd had the money regular. I ate four cream cakes and drank three coffees, and when the waitress brought the bill I grabbed it before Larry could get his hands on it. He shrugged and gave me a cigarette. 'You rob a bank or something on the weekend?'

That was one of the things I liked about him. He asked a question like that and if I'd said yes, he wouldn't have been the least bit bothered. I shook my head and told him all about Claire Kearney. As I went through the story he kept shaking his head in disbelief and at times he was laughing so much that I had to let him finish before I could go on. A lot of people sitting around were looking at him as though he was a head case, but it didn't bother him much.

'You're a terrible man,' he said. 'Honestly, I don't know where you'll end up at all.'

'What about Wicklow, though?' I said.

'I'd be gone by Tuesday, kid, but that's just my way. You're so young, you see. You could get her into serious trouble if it was found out.'

He was right there, of course. A thing like that in Ireland and you'd have every craw-thumper in the country down on your neck. What was taboo for them, you weren't going to enjoy. So Larry thought it best to leave it and just go down for the weekend whenever I could manage it. Also, he was so against getting involved that he was double wary of anything like that. 'Share yourself around' was his motto, 'give them all a break'.

He asked me what I thought of Breeda and if I'd enjoyed myself on Saturday.

'Terrific, Larry, the best time I ever had in my life. That Breeda's a lovely girl, isn't she?'

'She thought you were okay too,' he grinned. 'She didn't stop talking about you all evening.'

I liked him too much to try and see her behind his back, so I asked him straight out if it would be all right.

'Sure you can. She and I are just good friends,' he laughed. 'You know, screwing acquaintances.'

'She's great I know that much.'

'You keep on with the older ones,' he said, 'and if you're still alive by the time you're twenty you'll be the greatest lover in town. You can always learn something from older ones, and, anyway, kids are no good. You fight them to get it and after they've enjoyed it they cry their eyes out and expect you to marry them. I've no time for them myself.'

'Well, straight, Larry, I never thought I'd find it as easy as I've been doing. The way fellas talk, you'd think it was impossible to get a bit unless you went with a brasser. Honest, an awful lot of people'd be surprised at the number of virgins that aren't about.'

'This town's the same as anywhere else. Comparatively speaking, there's as much here as anywhere else.'

'Is Breeda really a masochist?' I said.

He was shaking his head again, not in answer but in sheer surprise. 'What do you know about things like that?'

'Ah, I read a few books about people like that, you know.'

'You're getting up on my back now,' he said. 'You never read books like that. Not in this country. The clergy and the rest of them see to that. After they've enjoyed them they decide that they're not fit for us to read.'

I should have known better than to kid Larry. He was too sharp. 'Ah, it's this friend I have in Rathmines. He knows all about that sort of thing.'

'Well, she is, as it happens. She gets a kick out of being hurt. Thing is, not to worry about it, try and look at it from her angle. It's the same to her as if you were stroking her headlamps. You enjoy that. She enjoys being hurt.'

'Oh, I'm not against it.'

'I didn't think you would be,' he grinned. We got up to go. 'She wants it,' he said, 'and if it's not you or me that gives it to her it'll be somebody else.'

'I'll do the best I can,' I said. 'It's no hardship, I can tell you.'

'One thing,' Larry said, 'if you do shoot off to the Garden of Ireland let me know where you are.'

'Ah, no, I won't go now. As you say, it's too risky.'

'Fair enough,' he nodded in agreement, 'but I just thought I'd mention it. You're so full of surprises that I thought I'd better.'

We went out into Grafton Street and with a wink he was gone and I was on my way back to the office. Cahill wasn't there when I got in and I was grateful for that. I made a quick phone call to Maureen because I hadn't seen her in her office when I'd been in on the delivery. I asked her if she was all right.

'Of course I'm all right. Why shouldn't I be?'

I was thinking of the nightmare and her having a kid.

'Don't be so silly,' she laughed into the phone. 'It's the exact opposite. It's my monthly, that's all. I'm always a bit rough for the first few days.'

After that I worked hard for an hour filing and copying proposal forms. I wanted things to be clear when Cahill came back, because it only needed the least thing for him to have a go at me and every day I was getting closer to punching him in the teeth.

Most of the girls were working hard at their machines. There was a busy hum in the room and it seemed good to be a part of it. Jack Sloane came up to my table and told me a joke. Poor Jack, he couldn't tell a joke to keep himself warm. He got it mixed up in the middle so that you knew what was coming before he finished, but I laughed my head off and he went back to his desk like he was topping the bill in the Theatre Royal.

When I looked over to the switchboard O'Boyle was purring down the phone at some university type who was after his corner and I wished that Cahill would come in just to see his face when he heard her. She had a laugh that was enough to bring you on and she knew it and never stopped using it. It was as if she started to laugh and then broke it in her throat, as if she really intended to growl at you. It really did something to me. Anyway, she kept on saying, 'Oh, Tony, you're awful,' until he must have started to believe it himself. Then Mr. Hayes came into the office and Tony got the fastest goodbye I've ever heard and she was all business, with her yes sirs and no sirs into the dead phone.

Two of the other girls exchanged a look, and a tch with the tongue and a flick of the eyes to the roof. They didn't like O'Boyle. She talked too often about all the men that were after her, which was bad enough, but even worse was the fact that they knew it was true. And she was always pulling up her stockings in public and the fact that she had beautiful legs didn't increase her popularity one little bit.

Every day I was beginning to fancy that O'Boyle a bit more. It was strictly for the other, mind you. I wasn't too keen on her apart from the idea of taking her to bed. She had too much mouth. All talk, as though she never got off her back, but it was odds on that if you dropped it into her hand she'd have passed out. A verbal sexo, that's what Miss O'Boyle was.

Mary Whelan was the best of the mots in the office. She was good-natured and she could listen to a joke once it wasn't too strong. And in her own quiet way she was nice-looking, and though she was always well covered up you could see she had a nice body. We used to cycle home together sometimes and when she pedalled I could see the top of her stocking and it looked nice and warm up there. She only talked to me like a big sister, though, and I liked her more than I did Josie. Still, if she'd been my sister she might have been different, just like Josie.

The firm was doing well. Every day business was on the increase. I was glad about that, the bosses were so nice and so good to their employees that they deserved to make money. And they encouraged us all to get business, promising half of the commission to anyone who did, which I thought was very fair. I tried hard and managed to get a couple of guys that I knew to insure their cars through the firm. The premiums weren't all that wonderful, and neither was my share of the commission, but it was a start and Mr. Hayes told me that he was pleased with my efforts.

That gave me a lift. I wanted Mr. Hayes to see something in return for the effort he'd put into me. He was a nice man and if he could see that I was really trying he wouldn't feel that he'd wasted his time on me.

At home on The Hill the fact that I worked in an insurance office was a sort of status symbol. Oul' ones said good evening to me with respect in their voices, and more than once someone came to the door to ask me to write a letter to the Corporation or the St. Vincent de Paul Society, or the like. At times like that Ma was very proud. You could see it in her walk and hear it in her voice and I got a thrill to see her that way. It was a good thing that she could be proud of me, even if I wasn't all that proud of myself.

12

Dᴜʀɪɴɢ that summer I grew a few inches, and thanks to all the Guinness I was drinking I filled out a bit in the body. And I began to get a real growth on my chin so that I had to shave a couple of times a week. As the fellas said, I was getting very dark around the gills.

I worked hard in the office and once I did so well in spotting a fake engineer's report on an old car that I got a few words of praise from Cahill. When he was congratulating me he was embarrassed and I realised that most of his arrogant, ignorant attitude was a cover-up for his shyness, and though I didn't like him any better I did try after that to make allowances when he took verbal liberties, and it wasn't so often that I felt the urge to put my fist in his face.

Up to the time the Technical School closed I went regularly, and thanks to this and all the reading that I did, and the scribbling into the exercise books and the endless talks with Redmond, from which I never failed to learn something, I was a lot wiser than I'd been on that first Monday at the office. And when I talked with Mr. Hayes I tried to let him see that I was working to improve myself. My word power was increasing, thanks to the word-a-day idea, and if I had a book in the office I'd leave it lying on the desk so that it could be seen. I didn't read Christie or Charteris. I had nothing against them but I just didn't have time to read strictly for pleasure. I had to learn something from each book, so that the literature that Mr. Hayes and the others saw lying on my table was what could usually be considered good gear. It wasn't a snob thing, I just wanted Mr. Hayes to see that he'd backed a winner. I kept myself neat and tidy as well and I don't think that anyone in the office, apart from Larry and Jack, knew that I took a drink.

Towards the end of the term in night school Maureen got a bit annoyed at the way I was concentrating on the lesson as opposed to her. I was interested in the subjects and I wanted to learn what I could, but she must have known that it wasn't just that. I found that I didn't have to keep touching her all the time. I knew that when we got out we'd go somewhere quiet and make love, so why muck about in the classroom. As I say, she must have sensed this in me because she was more possessive in the classroom than she was outside.

It wasn't that I'd gone off her. I loved her still. It was just a sort of taking-her-for-granted thing. I couldn't help it, and though she never once mentioned it I could feel that she resented it strongly. But I kept quiet about it, leaving well enough alone, and when we'd be walking along the street, and she'd stop to look in a window at a wedding gown or something like that, I didn't say anything either. If a subject isn't mentioned it's very hard to have a row about it.

We did a lot of walking, Maureen and I, and I'd almost completely stopped going to the films. Those days of Roy Rogers and all the others seemed far off and pointless, but I never regretted one moment of the time I'd spent watching them. They had filled a need at a bad time in my life and I'd never stop being grateful for that. Now it was drinking or whoring and talking and arguing that filled the time when I wasn't with Maureen or Breeda, or reading a book. It was a busy time with the job and the morning paper round, but I was rarely tired or depressed, except late at night on that journey up the hundred-yard laneway that led to The Hill. So with one thing and another it was mid-August before I finally got down to see Claire

Kearney in Wicklow, or, as Larry had called it that day in the coffee shop, The Garden of Ireland.

She had been phoning me once a week since she'd left Dublin and I was always promising that it would be the next weekend. At the time I really meant what I said, but by the Friday something would come up, like a bottle of Arthur J. Guinness or a fresh bird. And I kept putting it off.

It was diabolical considering how the woman felt about me and when you think of all the hours that she must have spent by the window, looking for the sight of me in the road, it was bloody nearly criminal. I knew how wrong it was and I kept on meaning to do something about it. It was a bit like that book I was going to write, but Maureen and Breeda were on the spot, giving me plenty of what I wanted, so Claire who wasn't so conveniently placed had to sit and wait.

Breeda had phoned me as Larry had said she would and I was like a dog on form the minute I heard her voice. It was soft on the phone, like the touch of her flesh, and from the off I was, as Larry would say, involved. I couldn't help it. I was crazy for her. So much so that once or twice I broke dates with Maureen, and I wanted so much to make Breeda happy that I got used to the idea of her wanting to be hurt. I was willing to do anything to keep her interested in me and even when she produced a whip I gave her what she wanted. I had to drink a half-bottle of Jameson's whiskey before I could do it and I never mentioned it to Redmond. He'd swallowed the yarn about the cane. It was a barefaced lie, but he'd believed it. Now I couldn't tell him something that was really true because I knew he'd laugh me out of the pub.

Larry warned me not to get too strongly attached to Breeda. He said she was a bit of a nut and likely to tell me to get out at any time. He tried to get it across on me that if that did happen it wouldn't be so hard on me, provided I wasn't in love with her. I listened but I didn't pay much attention. I couldn't help the strange kind of way that I felt about her. Right or wrong, it was a very strong thing as far as I was concerned.

A few times when Claire Kearney phoned from Wicklow I felt that O'Boyle was listening in, but as I was in a back office so that I could have a little privacy I couldn't be sure. Then she started putting it round the office that I was a bit of a ram, and from the way she said little things I knew that she'd heard Claire going on about needing me and all the rest of it. And when Claire talked like that you didn't need much imagination to guess exactly what it was that she did need.

It was at that time that the trouble between Maureen and me began. Breeda phoned, and though I had a date with Maureen for that same evening I couldn't stop myself going to the flat in Merrion Square. I told Maureen that I was working late and she said all right, though you could tell she didn't like it. One morning, after I'd broken a date with her, the woman who cleaned the office told me that a girl had phoned for me the night before. Right away I knew it was Maureen, but I didn't know what the hell to do about it. I'd already told the lie and she knew it and as it wasn't the first time she'd known I was kidding even as I'd been telling her. I cursed my own stupidity for not thinking that she might check on me and I wondered what would happen when I met her on the corner of Leinster Road.

Nothing happened, because she didn't show up for our date. I waited a whole hour, giving her five minutes and then another five, until in the end I went into Campion's feeling more than sorry for myself. How could she do it to me?

I drank more than my share and bought a few for Harry Redmond. I didn't talk much. I was so choked that it took me all my time to order the gargle. When I wouldn't buy any more for him Redmond got the needle and I ended up telling him to get lost before I kicked his teeth in. I'd never had a cross word with him until that night, and though he could have handled me with one hand he just drained his glass and walked out. He must have known that I was upset, although I hadn't said a word. Jeysus, I could never have admitted to Redmond that I'd been stood up by a mot! I'd never have heard the end of it.

When I left the pub I was footless, but I thought I'd walk up and see if Maureen was at home. She might be ill or anything. She probably hadn't stood me up at all. So I talked to myself but drunk and all as I was I knew I was kidding myself. I got across Rathmines Road somehow, but when I set foot in Leinster Road I knew I wouldn't get very far. I turned round to go home, but I was so drunk that I had to grab on to the railings and I must have been there for half an hour before I felt that I could walk.

I turned into Rathmines Road and I was getting along nicely when I saw Maureen get off the bus with Willie Egan. For a second I didn't move. Not Maureen, she wouldn't do that to me. Not bloody much she wouldn't.

They were laughing as they came towards me. I waited long enough to be sure she saw me, then I staggered across the road, my heart like a lump of sore blood, and me enjoying every second of the way I was suffering.

She shouted my name, but I didn't look back. I could tell how upset she was just by the way she said my name, but I kept going until her hand was on my arm. 'Paddy, please, wait.'

I shook her hand off with such force that she nearly fell over, and as I tried to walk off Egan spun me round and smashed his fist hard into the side of my head. I didn't see it coming and I went down very hard. The ground was spinning like a top and as I tried to get up on my feet most of the stout that I'd poured into myself came up, spewing all over the footpath. It would probably have come up anyway, I'd made such a pig of myself. Egan knocking me down that hard had just helped it along.

The blow hadn't hurt me all that much but I knew I'd been hit. Maureen was crying and at the same time ballocking the life out of Egan for hitting me like that. People were passing us by as if we were a few dustbins on the footpath. It wasn't unusual to see a fight on the stretch of road. Egan stood and took all that Maureen said. He was like a frightened rabbit and you could see that the poor bastard was crazy about her.

I was standing steady now, wiping my mouth with a hankie and taking deep breaths to try and clear my head. She watched me, still crying, and I felt bad about being the cause of her tears. Her eyes were too lovely ever to look raw. It was a sin to make her cry.

'I'm sorry, Maur. I didn't mean to make you cry.'

I turned to move off again, and when she reached out to touch me I moved aside. Egan put his hand out to hold me and I let him do it, knowing full well that he wouldn't hit me again, not after all that Maureen had said to him. Then as fast as I could I turned round and hit him between the eyes with my forehead. There was so much force behind the blow that I thought I'd fractured my skull. Egan stood there partly out, but without any hesitation I smashed my fist under his left ear and he went down like a sack of potatoes.

Maureen screamed, almost as though she knew I had a taste for blood, and it was only her pleading and the way she was hanging on to me that stopped me from kicking his head in. I was sick with meanness, so much so that for the first time in my life I wanted to put the boot into someone. And that included all the times I'd been beaten to a standstill in the everyday fights to and from school.

Those fights taught you one thing, if you hit someone hit him as though you mean to kill him. That way there's less chance of him getting up and of you having to hit him again. It's not nice and it's not sporting, but then fighting shouldn't be. And any man who fights voluntarily, without knowing that he can win, is a bloody fool. Which was why Egan came unstuck with me. He was big and hefty, probably thirteen stone in weight, and because of that and the fact that I was as skinny as a pencil he just took it for granted that he could put me out with a casual blow. And he learned that a fella of ten stone, who hits you right, can do a lot more damage than a fella of thirteen stone who doesn't know what it's all about.

I came to my senses and it was like coming out of a bad dream. For me it was always that way when I had a fight. You can learn the physical side of the thing, how to deliver a punch and the way to ride one and all the rest of it, but how do you learn not to vomit afterwards?

Maureen helped me lift Egan to his feet, and though I didn't expect it I was ready just in case he tried to land a crafty one. There wasn't any fight left in him. Even when he came round he was only half with it, and as soon as he felt he could walk, he staggered off without a word.

I felt sorry for Maureen. Me hitting Egan like that hadn't helped her at all. She would blame herself for being the cause of the whole thing when it was all my fault and nobody else's. There hadn't been any need at all for me to hit Egan. He'd only punched me because he was crazy about her and he'd thought that I was trying to hurt her when she grabbed my arm. And if he cared that much for her he couldn't have been all that bad a fella. But still, I thought, feck him, he hit me when I was too drunk to see it coming and what he got he asked for. And that was it. I accepted my side of the story, the one that showed me as the fella who'd been put upon.

'I wasn't waiting for you, Maureen. I'm sorry it happened.'

'Oh, Padd, you're such a bloody fool sometimes. I only did it because you let me down all those evenings. It's you I love. You know that.'

She stood there looking up at me and her lovely face all tear-stained and lined with worry. 'And I love you, Maur, but you'd be better off with him. He's your own age at least.'

There I was off again on the self-pity touch. And I thought that Breeda was a masochist. It wasn't enough that after all I'd done Maureen could stand there and tell me that she loved me. No, for me it had to be written down the centre of the Rathmines Road, in two-foot-long red letters. I love Paddy Maguire. He can do what he likes. He can walk all over me, but I love him and I don't care who knows it.

'Walk me home, Padd. I want to be with you. I can't help it.'

I tried to say no, to walk away from her. It would have been the decent thing to do, to leave her alone and give her the chance of finding someone who would treat her right. But I took her arm and walked in silence beside her. Soil everything, leave nothing untouched, put your mark on.

She stopped under the first tree we came to and she turned sharply to me and pushed her mouth against mine. It was so sudden that I don't think she'd planned it. I tried to resist the pull of her lips. Shag her, she went out with Egan behind my back. For about two seconds I tried, but it was no good. I was like Maureen, draining every shred of pleasure out of the kiss, and then I was pulling her after me into a garden, right there on the Leinster Road.

I put my old overcoat down and we lay on it and made love. It was an angry, wild thing to do, and we tore at each other, hurting and wanting so badly to be hurt. She tore my shirt open and bared her breasts against my chest, and without any thought of whether it was safe or not she drained me free of my need, shuddering violently beneath me on the old coat, not letting me escape. And we vowed love for ever and ever, and all that sort of rubbish.

For a few weeks after that we were great together. The fight with Egan had brought to the surface a depth of feeling that had been untapped before. Making love in that garden was the best I'd ever known with Maureen, and now there was greater tenderness than ever between us, and I loved her very much.

The feeling was so rich for a while that I tried to make myself quit seeing Breeda. It just didn't seem right to me to be having her, with Maureen so in love with me. But I couldn't stay away from her. All she had to do was phone me and I had no defence.

Twice a week we drank in the little boozer where I'd first met her and we usually went straight back to her flat for a session in the bed. Larry still saw her too, and he and I told each other all that we did with her, but Breeda never mentioned his name when I was alone in her company.

She didn't talk much about herself, but Larry had filled me in on part of her story. She was a civil servant and according to him she had degrees to burn. She must have had, because she spent so much money and she lived so well that her wages must have been a bomb. And in the civil service to earn the kind of money that she spent you'd have to be a right egg-head.

Larry said that a married man in her home town had put her in the puddin' club and that she'd left home then and gone over to England. And she'd had an abortion or a miscarriage or something, and had come back to Dublin. I often wondered if that was why she went all sad sometimes. It must be an awful thing for a mot to have to go through that kind of thing, especially if she's on her own. But Breeda never mentioned it and neither did I. As far as I was concerned she was a good skin and she never once mentioned how intelligent she was or anything like that. She just wasn't the kind of girl to wear it like a badge.

About six weeks after the fight with Egan, Maureen rang me one morning to cancel a date that we had for that night. She didn't give me any reason but she promised to tell me all about it the next night. I can't say why, but somehow I had the feeling that it was something to do with Willie Egan and when I thought about him I felt bad. I should never have hit him like that.

I met her outside Flood's pub in Terenure the next night, and she held my hand and we walked up in the direction of Temple-ogue. It was still fairly light, and Maureen was so quiet that I talked of weather and summer evenings. It struck me as fairly funny that after all we'd been through we seemed to be at a new beginning. It's odd that I should have thought that, just then. Before a new beginning there's always an end.

We walked for miles and we found a little country pub and in the bar there was an open turf fire, even though the night wasn't cold. And there were dark beams strung across the low ceiling and I thought that it would be a great place in which to sit and get quietly pissed.

Maureen asked for whiskey. No water or soda, just bottoms up, and it was then that my guts turned over on me. I knew from the way that she drank the spirit that there was something very wrong.

'You believe I love you?'

'Sure I do, Maur, what makes you ask that?'

Her voice was flat when she answered and her face was pale and drawn like a mask. 'I'm overdue with my monthly.' She looked at me and her eyes were sad enough to make the heart bleed. 'I'm going to marry Willie Egan.'

There was a mist across her eyes like a pain, and without thinking of myself, for once, I pitied her and I loved her. For a little while I was silent, not knowing what to say.

'It was that night in the garden, wasn't it?'

'Yes, it was. It was my fault, Padd, don't blame yourself. I started you off that night.'

'Does Willie know?'

She shook her head. 'Nobody knows but you.' She fiddled with the glass. 'I let him make love to me last night. He'll marry me tomorrow if I say yes.'

'But you don't love him.' As the stupid words tumbled out of my big mouth I knew it was a lousy thing to say. As if the poor cow didn't have enough on her plate, without my ego. She was angry when she spoke and you could hardly blame her for that.

'Of course I don't love him. How the hell can I when I'm daft about you. For Christ's sake, Paddy, don't be so stupid.'

'But you're definitely going to marry him.'

'Well, I can't marry you, can I?'

'No,' I could hear the hopeless ring in my own voice. 'You can't marry me.'

'Well, it's settled, then.'

She didn't say any more and I didn't know what to say. As usual I'd created a situation that I couldn't do anything about.

'Another drink, kid?'

'No. I just want to get out of here and go and lie down with you somewhere.' She smiled and I could see that she was heart-broken. 'It'll be the last time for us.'

And it was. The last time that I ever held on to her and loved her with my body, and I thought how marvellous she'd always been to me. Right from the off she'd been too good for me, and if I'd tried even to live up to her, the end wouldn't have seemed so bad and left such a rotten taste on my mouth.

I felt an awful lot older when we came out of the field, and when I kissed her goodbye and put her into a taxi I stood and watched until the car was out of sight. She was gone out of my life, and when she married Willie Egan a month later she carried a bit of me with her, in every sense of the word.

I saw her climb into the car outside the church, but I made sure that she didn't see me. She stood and smiled for the photo-grapher and she looked very happy. I stood, believing it was all an act, that she was torn asunder because it wasn't me that was getting into the car beside her.

For about a month after that I really did some hard drinking, and even on the nights that I saw Breeda I passed out before I could touch her. She didn't like it, and if I hadn't come around when I did I think she would have broken off with me.

When I felt all right I told Larry the whole story. He sat and listened and then he told me straight that I'd been very lucky to get out of it as I had done. Another bird would have lumbered me all the way, and apart from the fact that I'd have been married and me only just out of short trousers, it would have killed Ma, to see me shotgunned into a wedding. So, as Larry said, I'd been very lucky to escape with just a few bruises. It was just after that, in the middle of August, that I finally managed to get down to Wicklow to see Claire Kearney.

I was due a holiday from the office and I told Ma that I was going youth hostelling with some fellas that I worked with. She was delighted to hear that, glad that I would be getting fresh air into my lungs, and the fact that I was going with fellas from the office made it more than all right. Ma couldn't see any wrong in white-collar workers. Maybe that's why she thought so much of the clergy.

Breeda was a different problem, so I told her that I was going off for a week with my mother, that she hadn't been very well and that I wanted to try and give her a nice break for the seven days. She thought it was good that I cared so much about my mother, and I brought a few tears to my eyes and told her that Ma hadn't had much of a life and that I was only doing what I could to give her a rest. And Breeda was looking at me as though I should be canonised.

She asked me to stay with her on the Friday night before I left, so I told Ma that I was going to an all-night party from the office. Ma said it was all right and I knew she wouldn't worry about me. The word office had a magical effect on poor Ma.

Breeda had a terrific supply of gargle in the flat and we both got footless by about ten o'clock. It was a pretty stupid thing for me to do, and me faced with a sixty-mile bicycle ride the next afternoon. She seemed to expect a fortnight's sex in advance, so that it was about six in the morning when I finally closed my bloodshot eyes.

She woke me up at half past eight and I felt as though I'd been dead for a couple of years. I drank the black coffee that she made, and as I was going to be really late for the office she phoned for a taxi. I said I couldn't afford it and she was very decent about paying for it. So I arrived at the office in great style, but when Larry saw me he nearly threw a fit at the state of my eyes. 'Jesus wept. They're like pissholes in the snow. Breeda?'

I nodded and he grinned with that shake of his head that I'd gotten used to. 'Listen, kid, you'll kill yourself if you keep on like this. You'll have to slow down.'

'Don't worry,' I said. 'I'm slowing down whether I want to or not. I'm worn out.'

'You can say that again,' he said. 'Look, can you get out for coffee? You look like you need it.'

I nodded. 'I need something. You go on. I'll see you in about ten minutes. Okay?'

He nodded and went out of the office. Cahill wasn't in, thank the lord. It was his Saturday morning off and it made things just a bit easier for me. If he'd seen the state of me he'd have found something to keep me nailed to the desk all morning.

I went to Mr. Hayes' office and knocked on the door. His voice came through the glass panel and I went in.

'I'm sorry to trouble you, sir.'

'That's all right, Mr. Maguire. What can I do for you?'

'To tell you the truth, sir, I've been up all night. It's my sister, sir, she's not too well. I was out for the doctor just before I came to the office and I didn't even have time for a cup of tea. I was wondering, sir, if I could go out and get myself a sandwich?'

He looked at my face and he could only have been thinking that I looked dog rough, and fortunately for me he was a man who always thought the best of everyone. 'You do look rather tired, Mr. Maguire,' he said, and taking out his wallet he put a ten-bob note on the desk in front of me. 'A small gift for your holiday. Go out and get yourself a good breakfast.'

Believe it or not, I tried to refuse the money. I didn't want it, not after giving him such a load of bullshit, but he really did insist, and when I got to the coffee bar I was ten bob to the good.

Larry had a coffee waiting for me on the counter and I drank that down, followed by two more, and I began to feel a bit of life creep back into me. I told him what had happened with Mr. Hayes and he just put on his resigned expression.

'And me sitting here wondering if you'd even get out. Honest to Christ, it's you should be looking out for me.'

'It was an accident, Larry, I didn't want to con him for a half-note.'

'I know,' he said, 'that's just the point. When you're bull-shitting you believe every word you're saying, and poor fellas like Hayes just go for it. You can't lose.'

We had some more coffee and he told me to take it easy in Wicklow. I think he really was worried that I'd kill myself if I didn't watch it. And from the way I felt after spending the night with Breeda he was more than half right. Honestly, I felt that if a strong puff of wind came round the corner at me I'd take off like a bloody plane.

Ma had everything ready when I got home and she told me to hang on to my week's holiday pay. I was glad about that because I'd had to buy a few bits and pieces for the trip and I wasn't all that flush. Not that I ever had much money in my pocket. I spent too much on drink both for myself and Redmond. Funny, but though Ma must have known that I liked a drink it was something that was never mentioned between us. She didn't drink herself and she didn't approve of people who did, but for the pissy oul' fellas that lived in the flats she never ran any of them down. I think she felt that if it wasn't mentioned it was less likely to seem important.

As I checked the bike I couldn't help thinking of the way things had changed for me in such a short time. There I was with just over three quid in my bin, off for a week's holiday in the country, and I just felt okay about it. Yet only yesterday, or so it seemed, I was glad to earn a dollar for a twelve-hour day in the butcher's shop, or for a whole week's paper round. Now, a dollar to me was the price of a few drinks, and I thought that was bad. Not only was I drinking, I was getting to think like a drinker.

It was a good afternoon for the bike. The sun was warm, but there was just enough breeze to stop me from sweating too much. Poor Ma was hopping about like a hen on a hot griddle, worrying if I had this, that and the other. Not that there was much chance of me forgetting anything, the way she kept on.

I cycled down through Ranelagh and I felt great to be going off for a while. I didn't know what Wicklow was going to be like, but I didn't give a damn. Anything would be a nice break from The Hill and the scruffy kids and the oul' ones with their bags of turf for the fire, and the poor oul' fellas with the arses out of their trousers, and most of them twisted on a few pints. Not that there weren't a few 'well got' families in the flats. It was just that they seemed so out of place that it was difficult to think of them belonging there.

I worked my way down through Donnybrook. It was a nice little village, sort of oldey worldey, a place that should never have had to put up with petrol fumes and the rest. Horses and carts and ponies and traps and Donnybrook were as right together as tea and sugar. Next to Rathmines I liked it better than any other place I knew, and I remember in a pub one night a woman sang: 'He promised to take me to Donnybrook Fair, And buy me silk ribbons to tie up my hair.' An oldish woman she was, but she sang sweetly and she meant the words, although it was only a song.

The wheels of the bike hummed along the Stillorgan Road. It was a wide road and the surface was good and there weren't too many speed merchants about. God, I felt like a bird as I flew along and I hadn't a care. Not even the length of the journey ahead of me could cost me a thought. I was off for a week with money in my pocket to a warm reception from a woman who was waiting for me. It was a good day to be born.

At Blackrock I took to the coast road, going out on through

Seapoint and Dunlaoghaire, with the breeze from the sea coming up across the cottages, making my face as warm as sausages. And the wheels zipped along, eating up the road, and it was no effort and I was happy.

Just beyond Bray I rested on a grass verge and I drank a pint of Guinness that I'd stuck into the kitbag. I drank it too fast and it gave me a pain in my stomach, so that I had to sit for longer than I intended.

I didn't like Bray. It was all promenades and putting greens and amusements that had never amused anyone except the owners. A cup of tea cost more than it should have done and women queued up in the summer to go to the lavatory and I thought it a lousy place to go for a swim. Bray Head was okay if you wanted to lie down with a mot, but only at night. During the day it was like Moore Street market on Christmas Eve.

A lot of fellas that I knew raved about the place. A great place for picking up mots, they said, and the dances were supposed to be marvellous. But to my mind you were wasting your time unless you had a car to run them home. If you hadn't got a motor the mots that danced out there wouldn't give you the itch for fear that you might scratch it. And the fella with the most horse power got the girl with the biggest pair of bumpers. So, I couldn't see what was so hot about it. If you had money and a car you could get off with a mot on a desert island. As far as I was concerned Bray could be returned to the Leprechauns anytime, with apologies.

My shirt was sticking to the small of my back, and the rough trousers that I'd bought for a dollar in the army supply stores in Aungiers Street were hot on my legs. But I set off again and I couldn't have cared less. Wearing the old gear was saving the suit trousers, and that was the important thing.

I was riding through country now, fields and trees and me speeding along a ribbon of road that wound its way like a pale snake through the greenery. There were plenty of signposts and

I didn't have any trouble getting to Newtownmountkennedy. It was just as well that I was looking for it, though, otherwise I'd have gone through it and not known. It was only about the size of a big spit in the road.

It was a relief to get off the bike for a few minutes and I lit up a Woodbine. I wasn't a big smoker or anything like that, but it was something to do. Then I saw these two young fellas. About fifteen they were, playing pitch and toss by the roadside. I walked over and asked them for directions to Claire Kearney's place. Nice kids they were and they had a few bottles of cider lying in the grass where they were pitching. I gave them each a cigarette and took a drink of the scrump that they offered. They drank quite a bit, they said. All the girls left for Dublin or England as early as they could, and there wasn't a picture house for miles. So all they could do was was drink or play pitch and toss, or take one off the wrist. Without a picture house to while away the time you had to do something, they said.

When I got back up on the bike they went back to the pitch and toss. One of them tossed the coins into the air and the other drained a cider bottle. It didn't seem right to me that fellas of that age should have to drink to pass the time. I'd been a drinker at that age, but that was my own doing, and if it got me into trouble it was my own fault. But there didn't seem to be much justice if fellas of that age were driven to it just because there wasn't anything else to do.

13

CLAIRE was at the window when I pulled up outside the house. I wasn't surprised. It was an odds on bet that she'd been there all afternoon.

It was a beautiful evening and the house looked grand. It was laid out in two storeys and built into the side of a hill. It was well painted in a very pale blue, with a nice big front garden, long and wide and filled with all kinds of flowers. The sort of place that you would expect Claire to have, if you knew her.

She was at the door as I pushed the bike through the gate and she was blushing with pleasure, like a schoolgirl who had just won a prize. I kissed her and it was good to hold her after all this time and I could feel her warm tears on my face as we held on to each other.

'Oh, thank God, you've come!' was all she could say and I felt a right louse for having taken so long to get there.

She stood in the bathroom and talked to me as I soaked in the hot water and her eyes were alive as I dried myself with the towel. She must have seen the bruises on my body, but she didn't pass any remarks. I don't think it would have occurred to her that a woman had put them there.

She looked well, and though I was really knackered after the bicycle ride I couldn't resist the touch of her when she kissed me there in the bathroom. Her breasts bulged against me and she was fierce in her wanting, and it wasn't long before we were making up for all the weeks that we'd been away from each other.

And it was good and comfortable and much better than it had ever been in the house in Terenure.

The bed was soft and warm and I lay deep in the flock mattress while Claire went downstairs to bring up the Guinness and a tray of food. We didn't leave the bedroom at all that night. We just lay together and made love that was good, and I didn't wake up until I heard the birds singing on the Sunday morning.

After breakfast I went out and stood looking about the valley. It was a little way to one side of the main road that led into Aughrim and it was only a stone's throw from the Avonmore River. There was a patchwork quilt of fields, climbing up the sides of the valley. All shades of green, and the burnt brown leaves of a hundred trees made a natural pattern that had me holding my breath for the sheer beauty of it. And I thought of a word that I'd once seen in a catechism at school: tranquillity. That was something that the valley really did have, and I thought too that it was about as near to heaven as I was ever likely to get.

That was the first morning of one of the best weeks of my life. Seven days of all the things that made life worth while for me, and what made it even better was knowing that Claire was getting as much out of it as I was myself. Apart from one little row, after I'd made eyes at a young scivvie who was helping in the bar at the local pub, we didn't have a cross word.

The pub was three miles from the house, but it was the nearest one, so we went there a few times. Claire was known and told everyone that I was her nephew from Dublin. The barmaid fancied me strongly if her 'come and get me' eyes were anything to go by, and it wouldn't have been any hardship to have gone over the hurdles with her. Anyway, Claire was upset and she cried when we got back to the house. I convinced her that I was only acting, telling her that people would expect her nephew to make advances at the barmaid. She swallowed it and said she was sorry for being such a fool and we went to bed. I worked hard to assure her that I was in love with her, even though I was annoyed by the stupid tears and wishing that it was the barmaid with me in the bed and not Claire.

When she phoned and hired a car next day I was glad. I'd never been to Wicklow town and I was a bit fed-up with the house, and just a bit weary of Claire and her big tits. Little things that she did reminded me of the night Maureen had held my arm as though she'd owned it, and I felt hemmed in. I knew then why Breeda and I got along so well. She never took a liberty. She didn't want to be owned and she didn't expect to own anybody else, and the more you look the more you realise that there aren't many women like that about.

The car driver was an oul' fella with a face on him like a sod of turf and a voice like Mother Machree's illegitimate son. He wept and wailed about the cost of the juice for the car and the insurance premium and all the rest of it, and I thought that he had a bloody cheek to be going on like that and Claire paying for the hire of the car. Once or twice I nearly told him to put a sock in it, but Claire gave me a look that asked me to make allowances, so I let him get on with it.

When she bought me the suit and the two pairs of slacks I could hardly believe my luck. Then she got me some shoes and shirts and underwear. I put the grey pinhead on in the tailor's dressing-room and when I was all togged up I nearly cried. I was a fairly big fella now, getting a bit wiser every day, and I thought that I knew my way around better than most fellas of my age. And I had to go to Wicklow Town for a woman who was about twice my age to buy me my first set of underpants.

It was things like that happening that made me realise how underprivileged a lot of people are. I don't just mean myself. I was very lucky, but all fellas should have underpants from the time they're kids, and all girls should have knickers and brassières and whatever else they wear. And people should be able to have a bath every day if they want to. It's just not right that people should have to suffer the indignity of being dirty or without underwear. We should either all be naked or all be decently dressed from the skin outwards.

I admired myself in the full-length mirror in the shop. The suit might have been made for me, and with the white shirt and the maroon tie I looked really well. Claire raved: I was so very handsome and my features were so good and there was such a shine to my hair. I couldn't see what she was on about, but I didn't argue. She had a certain picture of me in her mind and as far as I was concerned she was welcome to it. If I'd told her that I was a pale-faced bastard and not worth two pennyworth of cow-dung it would only make me seem even more romantic.

We had a meal in an hotel after leaving the shops and then we sat drinking in a modern bar that seemed out of place in a town like Wicklow. By the time we got back to the car I had cow-dung on my new shoes, but I was too pissed to worry about it, and to shut up Ballocky Bill the Driver I sang all the way back to the house.

Claire said I had a lovely voice and your man at the steering wheel cried his eyes out when I sang 'Daddy's little girl'. He had two daughters in America. They were married and raising herds of little American citizens. I wished I'd never opened my mouth, but I sang 'Kevin Barry' to shut him up. Even then he started on about 'the troubles', but I kept on singing, trying as hard as I could to lift the roof off his shagging car.

The singing did one useful thing. It gave me a story as to how I got my hands on the new clobber, and when I got home to Ma I was going to need one. I'd won a talent contest in one of the hostels and the prize had been a voucher for fifteen pounds. It would take some telling, that I did know. Fifteen quid was a lot of dough and while Ma might believe me Josie would take a lot of convincing. Not that I cared what she thought, it was just that Ma would be happier if Josie believed me too.

I didn't say anything to Claire about it and it never even occurred to her that I'd need a story. She didn't think like that because she didn't have to, and she was lucky. But for me it was second nature. It seemed that all my life I'd had to tell lies about something or other, and if I was good at it it was only because I'd had so much practice.

When Saturday came I was relieved, but I acted as heartbroken as Claire obviously was. She was so full of grief that I was sorry for her. She kept on about her age and how tragic it was that I was so young, that I could never really belong to her—'my new owner is Claire Kearney'—and that I'd forget her as soon as I was back home again.

I tried to make her believe that I'd never forget her, but she wouldn't stop crying, and again I felt the urge to punch her in the face. But I didn't do it. I acted my head off and it was good practice for the way I'd have to perform over the new suit when I got home. And by the time I finished she seemed a lot better.

She packed all my stuff in a suitcase that I didn't want. Then I thought I'd throw that in with the story about the gear. In for a penny in for a pound. The case felt strange in my hand as I carried it to the door. I kissed her goodbye and she cried again. I told her that I loved her and it was then that she put the two fivers in my hand.

'God, Claire, you're awful good to me. Thanks a million, and I promise I'll get down again as soon as I can.'

'Please God you will, Paddy. I don't know what I'll do without you. I'll never forget this past week. You made me very happy.'

I nodded and kissed her again. She was a nice woman and she deserved a better life than she was having. Her money couldn't buy her a man she could love, it couldn't even buy her a bag of bones like me. I said goodbye to her again and then I was away down the road, with the suitcases across the handlebar of the bike and the two fivers in my trouser pocket, burning like a lump of hot turf against my leg.

With ten pounds you could buy two suits, or a bicycle, or if you looked at it the other way it was two week's pay for a lot of men, or it would get you about two hundred pints of Guinness. Whatever way you thought about it it was a lot of dough and it was in my trouser pocket, and I had about as much intention of cycling home to Dublin as I had of becoming a Jesuit.

I got on the train at Wicklow and the guard put my bike in his van. There wasn't anybody else in the carriage so as we pulled away I stretched out on the seat, and the next thing I knew the guard was shaking me by the shoulder to tell me that we were in Dublin. And that's the way to travel, I'll tell you.

When he came back with the bike from his van I gave him a shilling, and he was as surprised as I'd been when Claire had handed me the two fivers.

'The blessin's 'a God on ye, sir. Many t'anks.'

He was still standing there looking after me when I got to the end of the platform and I was delighted to have made his day for the sake of a shilling. It was a great feeling to be able to give things to people. It made you feel like a king.

It was only half past one when I got out on to the street, which meant it was too early to go home if I was supposed to have have cycled. So I parked the bike and went into a boozer, and I ordered a pint of stout and a beef sandwich. The case was by my feet on the floor and I had a quick count-up while I waited for the pint to come up. Apart from the tenner, I still had best part of the money I'd taken away with me. Twelve pounds fifteen, all told, and it took some getting used to, to be sitting there with all that in my pocket.

An oul' fella who'd been sitting at the bar got up and went out, and the door hadn't stopped swinging behind him when the woman came in. She was a blonde and as beautiful as anything I'd ever seen. She looked hard but if anything this enhanced her looks and I couldn't take my eyes off her.

She leaned against the bar and she turned then and looked at me. I was wearing the heather-coloured suit, which still had a bit of life left in it, so I wasn't worried about my appearance. It was the way she looked that gave me confidence, as though she was saying 'Make a move'.

'Will you join me for a drink?'

She smiled and you could see that she expected me to say just that. 'Thank you, love. I'll have a gin and it with you.'

I stood up, liking the dry flat voice. The barman came back with my pint and I ordered her drink. She walked over to the table where I'd been sitting and I thought what a pleasure it was to meet a woman who knew just how good she looked. While I was waiting for her drink at the bar I stood looking at her and her eyes were on my face. When I took the drinks to the table she moved up a bit on the bench seat and I sat beside her.

'Just passing through, are you?'

Her voice wasn't what you would call common, but the flat, matter-of-fact way she spoke was very Dublin.

'No,' I said, 'I'm just back from holiday.'

'And down to your last few bob, I suppose.' It was more of a statement than a question.

'No,' I said, in my innocence, 'I still have a couple of quid left.'

She sat a bit nearer to me. 'You're a very nice-looking fella. Have you ten bob to spend on a nice afternoon?'

'How do you mean?'

I wasn't trying to be funny. Up to that moment I still hadn't fallen in.

'I'm a working girl, love. Ten shillings to you.'

I couldn't believe it, not with her being so lovely. I'd seen prostitutes before but they were mostly old and rough-looking and usually drunk. I'd never been with one. They were for fellas with money and with the way I drank I didn't have any for the mots. Not that I was bothered. With my luck I'd never had to pay for it. But this one was different. She was one of the

155

most striking-looking women I'd ever seen and I wanted to see what she was like. And I was in a position where ten bob didn't matter at all.

'Sounds great,' I said. 'What's your name?'

'Mary,' she smiled, and her teeth were clean and even in her mouth. 'After the Blessed Virgin.'

She drained the glass and stood up. 'Come on round to the house. It's not far.'

I stood up and lifted the case and she gave me a smile. 'I promise you you'll get your money's worth.'

I followed her out of the pub. The bike was where I'd left it and I thought to hell with it. It was insured against theft and at that moment I couldn't have cared less about it. She opened the door of a small terraced house and I followed her in as if I was the new lodger. I must have been mad. For all I knew the place might have been full of people, including her husband, but the way I was feeling at the thoughts of having her didn't help me to be logical.

'Don't worry, love. We have the place to ourselves.'

I followed her into the downstairs front room. It was clean and bright and there was a couch bed already made up. I put the case down and she locked the door behind me. She took off the small black jacket of her costume, and then with her eyes on my face she took off her blouse.

Her breasts were bare and didn't need any support, and I just stood there looking. She walked over to me and put her arms around me, and when I kissed her I could feel her breath go in with the force of my lips. She moved against me and her tongue found mine and when she broke away I almost ripped my clothes off. Then we were together on the bed, and she was fantastic in her love-making. It was half past six when we got up to dress.

I gave her the ten shillings and she kissed me again. 'You're very nice,' she said. 'Come and see me again.'

When I left her I went round and picked up the bike. I was a

156

bit surprised that it was still there. It was the old story of not worrying and nothing happens. Anyway, after the session I'd just had with Mary, or whatever her name was, I was glad that it was only a ten-minute ride home to The Hill, I was knackered.

Ma was delighted to have me back, but I was hardly through the door when she started on about me not being sunburned.

'Ah, you know me, Ma. Oul' paleface. Hello, Mrs. Doyle.'

'Hello, Paddy, was it a good time?'

She was Ma's best friend for thirty years and as sweet an oul' one as ever drew breath.

'Oh, a gift, Mrs. Doyle. Lovely altogether.'

Ma was eyeing the case when Josie came in from the lavatory.

'Hello, trouble.'

'Hello, sister. How's every little thing?'

Mrs. Doyle hid her mouth with her hand. She didn't want Josie to see her laughing. Josie put on a Buddy Clark record. He was her favourite singer.

'Where'd you get the case, son?'

This is it, I thought. Boy, you better make it good.

'Don't worry about the case, Ma. Wait till you see what's inside it. Your eyes will pop.'

I lifted the case and put it on the table. Ma and Mrs. Doyle had their eyes on my fingers as I undid the catch. Josie stood listening to Buddy Clark. She didn't want me to think she was interested, but she was. I threw the lid back. 'And now, ladies and gentlemen, you've seen a rabbit come out of a hat, but look here.' I lifted the suit jacket out and held it against myself.

'Isn't that beauty-full,' Mrs. Doyle said.

Then the rest of the stuff and the look of surprise on Josie's face. 'And now for my next trick, ladies and gentlemen.'

'Where did they come from?' Josie just beat Ma to it.

'I knew it, folks, I just knew you'd ask me that.' Boy, was I trying. 'So on the long journey home on the bike I beat my brains out, trying to come up with a convincing lie.'

'Oh, Paddy, you are a lad,' said Mrs. Doyle.

Buddy Clark finished his song and got switched off. Josie had her teeth in. 'Tell me where you got them, son?' Ma was only worried in case I'd nicked them.

'So, ladies and gentlemen, I am going to tell you the truth.'

'He pinched them.'

'Josie!' Ma spun on her and Josie shut up.

'I won them in a talent contest,' I said.

'A talent contest?' Ma said.

'Well, isn't that wonderful,' said Mrs. Doyle.

'Doing what?' Josie said.

'Singing.'

'Singing?'

'Singing,' I said again, 'and none of that buh buh buh buh, like that eejit there.' I nodded at the record of the great Buddy Clark. He was a favourite of mine, though I'd never let Josie know. 'The real stuff. Straight out, you know, "I'll take you home again, Kathleen," you know.'

'You're not fit to wipe his boots,' Josie said.

'He doesn't wear boots, he wears suède shoes.' I tried to make her angry. When that happened she forgot everything.

'That's enough, both of you. Son, is that the truth?'

'Well, not really Ma. It was a fifteen-pound voucher for clothes that I won.' I shut the case. 'And I bought what's there and the secondhand case as well.'

'It's better to be born lucky than rich,' Mrs. Doyle said.

'Oh, it wasn't luck, Mrs. Doyle, it was talent.'

'Oh, I know Paddy, I only meant——'

'Ah, I was only kidding, Mrs. Doyle. I know what you meant.'

Ma sat down and Josie turned on the record-player again. Then I pulled my big stroke. 'There y'are, Ma.' I put two pound notes on the table. 'You can have that, I hardly spent anything.'

'Well, glory be,' Mrs. Doyle said.

Ma picked up the two notes and I knew I was home and dried.

Even Josie was convinced. I knew it by the way she turned down the sound of the record.

'Thanks, son. There y'are, Mrs. Doyle,' Ma said, handing her one of the notes. 'That'll keep you going till Tuesday.'

'Oh, the blessing of God on you, Mrs. Maguire, and on you too, Paddy.' She put the pound in her purse. It would help her out until she got her husband's money from the Army. I picked the suit up off the table to hang it in the old wardrobe.

'It's a nice suit,' Josie said.

I turned to her. 'Shall I give you a song?'

She smiled, despite herself, and I think that for just that moment we really loved each other. 'Ah shurrup,' she said, 'I'm trying to listen to Buddy.'

'Who, him?'

She grinned at me, knowing that I was kidding, and I went into the bedroom.

When I came back out I knew that I could do no wrong. I'd come back and they were glad to see me and once they knew that I hadn't done anything that would get me into trouble they were happy. And the two pound notes had been like a breath of fresh air.

By the time I'd finished shaving Ma and Mrs. Doyle had gone off to The Stella to see *The Jolson Story*. Al Jolson was a big favourite with both of them. They'd stood together to see him in *The Singing Fool* all those years ago. I was chuffed for the pair of them and even though I'd given the two quid for the wrong reason I was glad that I'd done it. They'd get a few hours, enjoyment above in the picture house and they'd have enough for food for the weekend. And I wouldn't feel so bad about hanging on to those two fivers.

14

O N T H E way up to Campion's I remembered the first night
I'd worn the tweed suit, and how I'd felt as I'd walked up
through Gulistan Cottages with just a few shillings in my pocket.
Or was it a couple of quid? It was hard to be sure as I stepped it
out in the grey pinhead, with the two crispy fivers in the inside
pocket of my jacket.

I thought about luck too, and the way I seemed to attract it.
There was no accounting for it, but everything I did seemed to
work out right for me. And even when things went against me,
like with Maureen and the baby, I got off with little more than
a flesh wound. If I'd been able to believe in God I'd have said
that there was a guardian angel looking after me, but with the
way I lived that didn't make sense. Unless God knew how I felt
about things and accepted me as I was, but that didn't make
sense either. According to the books and the priests, God was the
top man, and unless you played it strictly by the rules he had
no time for you. By the time I got into the bar I hadn't come
up with the answer.

Poor Redmond. I always seemed to be making him green
with envy, and as he stared at the suit I wondered why he ever
bothered with me at all. It couldn't have been easy for him and
him still wearing the suit with the shine on it. I know that if it
had been the other way round I'd have found a new pub to
drink in.

He was in company, but he got up and walked over to me as
I stood waiting for the two pints I'd ordered.

'Tell us how you do it, Maguire. Just tell us how in the name of Jeysus you do it?'

'What are y'on about now?'

'The clobber, the clobber. What the fuckin' hell do you think I'm on about?'

The barman put the drinks in front of me and I handed him one of the fivers. Redmond looked from the note to me and back again. He didn't say anything, but he looked as though he was about to bang his head against the wall. Then he grabbed the pint and put it straight down in one swallow. 'Two more, Jimmy,' he called to the barman. He looked hard at me for a second. 'You know, Maguire, I was more right than I knew when I christened you golden ballocks. How in the name of Jeysus do you do it? And don't tell me it was the masochist with the cane that paid you for beating the arse off her or I'll drop dead where I stand.'

I pulled out a packet of Woodbines and gave him one. He even looked at that as though it was a thirty-shilling cigar.

'It's only a Woodbine, Harry, for Jeysus' sake.'

He grinned at me, recovering his sense of humour. 'Sure, but I was just checking. If it was marijuana I wouldn't blink a lid.'

We lit up and I paid for the second two pints. I hadn't even started on the first one, so I carried two over to the table. We sat down and I put a big hole in one pint. If I didn't Redmond would end up drinking mine and all.

'And it's not a cane any more, either,' I said. 'It's a whip.'

'Ah, for Jeysus' sake, Maguire, couldn't you put us in just once? Couldn't you?'

'I can't, Harry. She's not that kind of a mot. She likes me. She won't do it just for anybody.'

'Was it her gave you the clobber and the fiver?'

I shook my head. 'No. I won the suit and some other gear in a talent contest.'

'Ah, Maguire, for God's sake, will you leave off. This is Redmond you're talking to, remember. There's no need to get up on me back altogether.'

'Straight, Harry. I sang a couple of songs in a talent contest and I won first prize.'

'I never knew you could sing.' He was a bit doubtful.

'Well, I didn't print the money myself and I didn't pull the suit off a bush either. Will you believe that?'

'What about the fiver, then? Where did that come from?'

'The mot. I've been down with her in Wicklow for a week.'

He was impressed. 'Right enough,' he said, 'I haven't seen you around all week.' He rubbed his jaw viciously. 'The one with the whip? Was it?'

I nodded. 'Yeh, she gave me the time of my life and then threw me the fiver when I was leaving.'

'You're poxed in luck.' He spat the words out like bullets. 'All my life I've been looking for a bird with dough, and a no-good bastard like you gets one with no bother.'

'Well,' I said, 'you're the one that put me up to it. It was you who told me to go into insurance and meet people. That's how it all started.'

He nodded his head like an old man and I burst out laughing. 'Why do you think I buy you all the gargle I do. You don't think it's because I like you, surely to God.'

'If you bought me a barrel a day, boy, you couldn't pay me back for meeting a bird like that.' His eyes went vacant. 'A masochist with money. Jeysus, all this and heaven too!'

I left him there drooling and went over and ordered two more pints. He still sat dreaming at the table, and I thought that if the suit had made him envious the bullshit was at least giving him a bit of pleasure. He wasn't having it himself but he knew someone who was, and to Redmond that was better than nothing.

For the next half-hour he kept on about the talent contest, but I stuck to my story. It was a lie, but if I were to tell him the truth he'd only hate me twice as much for being the luckiest bastard that ever drew breath.

When he suggested going into town for a drink I said okay. I had money to burn and I was in the humour for a change of scene, so in no time at all we were getting off a bus in Parnell Street.

He took me into a big lounge that was well filled with people, including women. That was something I hadn't expected. You just didn't see all that many women in pubs in Dublin. There was a fat fella playing the piano in one corner. His hands tickled the keys beautifully and he was all smiles; and there was a microphone beside him. He had a nice sort of a face and he seemed so happy that you couldn't help liking the look of him, and the feeling that everyone was having a good time was very strong in the room.

I bought a couple of whiskies and two pints of stout and when I handed Redmond the small glass he licked his lips. He took the whiskey in his mouth and he rolled it around his tongue. Not getting much chance to drink 'the hard tack', as he called it, he wasn't just slinging it down the hatch.

It was a big lounge and newly decorated and there was a man in a grey suit behind the bar, who looked like the boss. He kept an eye on the six hard-working barmen and he seemed very pleased with the way the bells on his tills were steadily ringing. And you could hardly blame him. The barmen couldn't pull the drinks quick enough.

'Good evening, ladies and gentlemen.' The fat pianist was on the microphone. 'We start the ball rolling this evening with a song from your friend and mine, Tommy O'Reilly. And remember, ladies and gents, respect for the singer at all times and, of course, the microphone is open to everyone. A big hand now, please, for Tommy O'Reilly.'

There was a good deal of applause for the man who walked up to the piano. He was a stout little fella of about fifty, and he

163

had the easy way about him of a man who had done it all before. He wasn't shy or nervous and when he began to sing it was in a good strong 'Peter Dawson' voice. He didn't pay any attention to the microphone. He didn't need it, and when he finished the audience nearly brought the house down with applause. Then, for his encore, the little man did 'Me and My Shadow', in a song-and-soft-shoe-dance routine, and I thought he was great. He worked hard and he was enjoying every second of it, and when I glanced at Redmond I could see that he was lapping it up as much as I was.

After that it was a long procession of people up to the microphone. Some were good, others not so good, but every one of them having a try, giving a little of themselves and having fun as they did so. That was the great thing about it, as far as I could see. Everyone wanted to contribute something towards the success of the evening, and though I kept on looking about the room I didn't see one person pull a face if one of the singers hit a bad note. Getting up and having a go seemed to be all that mattered.

By the time we'd had four or five rounds Redmond was looking really smug about something. I was trying to find out why without actually asking him when the pianist asked me by name, over the microphone, to 'oblige the company'. I knew then why Redmond had brought me to a singing house.

'This'll be a cakewalk after winning a talent contest,' he said slyly, with a grin on his bloody crooked mouth.

I felt like running out of the door, but I knew he was waiting for me to do just that. 'You sleeveen bastard,' I hissed at him, and I walked up the room to the piano, my legs like jelly and my insides turning over with nerves.

I always think of that first walk to the piano whenever I hear people run down a singer or a comedian. It always seems so easy, when you're just watching, to do so much better. All you have to do is stand there. Well, I stood there as the pianist played my introduction, and from the way my legs were shaking it took me all my time not to fall down on the floor. And all the nice people that had been in the room before were gone. Instead, there was a great number of vicious faces, all waiting for me to make a ballocks of myself. And when a fella sneered to his mot he was sneering at me. I knew he was, I just knew it.

I picked a spot on the wall, just below the ceiling at the back of the lounge, and I sang to that. I couldn't look at the faces around me. If I did I knew that I'd never get through the song.

At that time Billy Daniels had made a great record of 'Bye Bye Blackbird', and I sang it as I'd learned it from the record. And instead of just standing and shaking all over I began to move the way he did. It worked well for me. So much so that I dragged my eyes down off the wall and began to roll them to help my performance. Then I could see that the faces were all interested and one or two people gave me nods and winks of encouragement, and suddenly I wasn't nervous and it was a great feeling.

For an encore I sang 'Patsy Fagan'. This is an Irish comic song about a fella who goes labouring in Glasgow. The sort of number that you can fool around with, and when I finished I knew from the applause that it had gone down well. When I got back to Redmond I could see that he was more than a bit surprised, and I thought it was just as well, because I hadn't got over the whole thing myself.

'You did all right, boy. Not too dusty at all.'

And I'll tell you one thing, from Redmond that was praise indeed, and I bought another two pints on the strength of it.

From that night on we did very little drinking in Rathmines. I dragged poor Redmond all over Dublin, from one singing house to another, singing in each one and getting more confident all the time. Harry cursed the night he'd started me off, moaning like hell about the drinking time that we lost as we made our way from one pub to another, but I didn't pay much attention to him. I knew that as long as I was buying the gargle Harry would keep me company.

Singing, if you could call it that, had become very important to me, and apart from the time I spent with Breeda I did little else. No reading or scribbling in exercise books, and the dream to write was in a trunk in an attic in the back of my mind. Not dead but sleeping.

I didn't say anything about the singing at home. I was afraid that Ma would worry herself to death if I openly admitted that I was in pubs most nights of the week. Also, Josie would have laughed herself sick at my expense, and Billy would have sniffed and made some remark, probably true, that would have caused a fight. I just couldn't see them understanding me wanting to sing more than I wanted to work in insurance.

Even Redmond would have laughed if I'd told him that I wanted to be a singer. To his mind it was okay going around the pubs and singing a few songs over a couple of drinks, but fancying yourself enough to think you could go on a real stage and get paid for it, that would have seemed a bit strong to him. It was something that he would never have attempted; Redmond was a born talker, a fella who could tie most people in knots with words, but he didn't talk so well without a glass in his hand; in cold sobriety he was a bit shy, unless he was talking to such an eejit that he felt superior. And, as he said himself, the only thing wrong with his voice was the bloody sound of it.

So once again it was to Larry Deegan that I turned for advice. He was the one person I knew who wouldn't be surprised at anything I might say, and more than once since my return from Wicklow and Claire he had asked me if I was okay. He felt a change in me, he said. Was I fed up with the office? And he said this more and more, just about the time I decided to try my hand at singing.

I'd told him about the suit and the money and the way I'd kidded at home about the talent contest. And in the little pub where we drank we'd gone over the story so many times that we'd milked it dry of every laugh that was in it. Now he listened as I told him about the singing houses and the way that I was able to work a number, and it wasn't long before he realised how much I enjoyed entertaining people.

'I think you could be anything you want,' he said. 'And whether or not you're a great singer doesn't matter. You have enough appearance and personality to put over a song. That's all that counts now. If it wasn't for microphones you wouldn't be able to hear Crosby and the rest of them behind a tram ticket.' And I knew he was right. Microphone technique was just as important as singing, and it seemed to me that this was something I had. And I would always be a 'mike' man because I was a crooner, if I was anything.

That Thurdsay night I went with Redmond to a place called Hollyfield Hall above in Terenure. Thursday was talent-contest night, and after I'd sung a couple of songs the man in charge asked me if I'd sing in a charity concert on the Sunday night. I was delighted. There was no money in it but it was a chance to sing on a real stage before a big audience, and for once even Redmond seemed enthusiastic.

On Sunday at about nine o'clock I died on that stage, and it was something that I'll never forget in my life. The microphone broke down, the pianist messed up my accompaniment and to put the tin hat on it there was a fella in the front row who could sing ten times louder than I could. And the bastard did just that, believe me. Honest to God, I felt like jumping feet first into his big mouth, but all I could do was struggle through the number. I got a bit of applause that was pure sympathy, and as I walked off the stage I felt about nine inches high.

Redmond put an arm round my shoulder as I got off. 'Don't worry, boy, you did all right, considering.'

He turned round to the fella in charge who had just come off the stage after announcing the next act. 'You're a right prick,' he said in a loud voice. 'You invite the kid up here to sing and he doesn't get a bit of help from any of you. Not from you or the pianist or anyone else.'

'Sssh,' the man hissed, 'there's a show going on out there.'

Redmond laughed straight into his face. 'Go take another look, you might change your mind.' He turned to me. 'Come on, kid, let's get out of this kip.'

I followed him out, and though I knew he was right about me not getting any help it wasn't much consolation. And I could remember reading that every stage performer that ever lived was supposed to have gone through a similar experience, but that didn't help either. What happened to them and what happened to me were two entirely different things, and I was fairly heart-sore when we got to a pub and went in for a drink.

Like everything else I got over it in a few days and I kept on at the pub-crawling. And sometimes when I thought about the concert I was glad of the experience. The fact that I could want to go on with the singing after that meant that I believed in myself enough to put up with any hardship that might come along as I tried to make my way. And that was a good thing, I felt.

One thing that did bother me, though, was the change in my attitude towards insurance. I wasn't worried about being fed-up with the paper round, that had always been strictly for the much needed money, but insurance had been my life for all those months. And now, suddenly, I couldn't bear the thought of going into the office. Even a promotion from office boy to junior clerk didn't strike a chord of enthusiasm in me.

I was grateful when Mr. Hayes told me the news, and to tell the truth it was much sooner than I had expected it, but it wasn't important any more. The ten-bob rise was a great help, but I didn't care whether I was to deliver letters or dictate them in the office. All I wanted to do was to get out of there and try and earn a living on the stage.

For Ma, though, it was a marvellous Christmas present. She

danced around the kitchen when I told her the news and even Josie told me that I couldn't have been as stupid as I looked. Breeda was pleased for me too, thinking it was what I wanted. I hadn't ever mentioned the singing to her, for though we did things to each other each week we didn't talk much about ourselves. The two things just didn't seem to go together.

In January I got three small parts in an operetta that was being performed out in Clontarf. It was *Gypsy Love* by Lehar, and apart from missing one entry, through day-dreaming side stage, I did all right. It was good experience to have to do things with a lot of other people, and as there was always a decent drink in the dressing-rooms I really enjoyed myself.

Then through answering an urgent advert in *The Independent* I got a one-night stand with a fifth-rate dance band. We left Dublin at six in the evening and drove to the back of beyond, not getting there until nine o'clock. The dance started at ten and went on until four, and it was the hardest work I'd ever done in my life.

We had no rehearsals at all, so the bloke who ran the band told me to sing the ones I knew after the first chorus had been played. Well, I must have sung a hundred numbers that night, and by the time I got home at eight in the morning I had lost my voice completely, so that I'd really earned the three and a half quid that I'd been paid. But I was happy with the way things had gone and I'd been promised more work with the band in the future.

Doing that gig, as it was called, gave me a real taste of what I wanted to do, and going into work in the office became even harder. The work was interesting and I was soon dictating letters about glass claims and I was given small employers' liability cases to handle. I got on well at it, liking the business of dictating letters and talking to all kinds of people, both on the phone and at the counter in the office.

It wasn't long though before Cahill and myself were at each

other's throats about the way I worded my correspondence. He still insisted on the old stereotyped letter and I wanted to use a bit of imagination based on the way the English teacher and the commerce teacher at the Technical School had taught me. It got so bad that he reported me to Mr. Hayes after I had told him to his face that he didn't know a bee from a bull's ballocks.

I felt bad to be standing in front of Mr. Hayes, knowing that he was upset and angry with me. 'Well, Mr. Maguire, what do you have to say?'

'I'm sorry, sir, I lost my temper. It's just that it seems so old-fashioned, the way Mr. Cahill wants me to write. I was taught at night school that the way I've tried to do it is better and much more economical in every way.'

He didn't like it, I could see that, but to give him his due he tried to be fair.

'Mr. Cahill has been in insurance a great number of years now, Mr. Maguire. Is that to count for nothing, just because you think he may be wrong about certain things?'

'No, sir.'

'Very well, then. I want you to apologise to Mr. Cahill.' He could see me go stiff. 'Whether you were right or wrong in your opinion, Mr. Maguire, you were wrong to speak to the office manager as you did. You will apologise?'

Even then he gave me a choice, although really it amounted to telling me. 'Yes, sir,' I said, sweat standing on my face.

Cahill came in and he had a smug look on his clock that made me clench my fists behind my back.

'Ah, Mr. Cahill. Mr. Maguire wishes to apologise for his outburst. Will you accept his apology?'

Cahill nodded, smiling, and Mr. Hayes looked at me. 'I'm sorry, sir,' I said to Cahill.

'Apology accepted,' Cahill said, in his magnanimous voice. 'I'm sure it won't happen again.' He looked at Mr. Hayes.

'It won't, sir,' I said, hurting myself to push the sentence out.

I was allowed to back out to the other office then and I was fit to commit murder. I didn't mind Mr. Hayes telling me off. I would willingly have let him kick me around the street sooner than apologise to the other bastard, but what could I do? When it came down to it I was about as important in that office as a broken filing cabinet.

That incident put the last nail in the coffin. Now I knew that if I didn't get out soon I'd get the sack. I didn't want trouble, but I knew that I couldn't go on doing something that I felt was wrong, and the way Cahill wanted me to dictate my letters made me sick. And if it hadn't been for Ma I'd have been out that very day. I could have found the guts not to apologise, but I didn't have enough to go home and tell Ma about it afterwards. So I began to resent my mother and that made me sadder than I'd ever been.

15

I DRANK more than ever from that day on and I had no interest at all in my work. Cahill probably thought I was knuckling down, but it wasn't that. I was biding my time and meanwhile I did what he expected me to do. We had no more arguments. My mind was a blank and I just went through the motions of the job like a zombie.

Redmond and I still drank all over town, and I was one of the regular turns in numerous pubs. And we began to get friendly with all kinds of people and we made a good team. I was regarded as a fella who liked a drink and was fun to have around the place, especially if there was a party on, and Redmond, in shiny suit, was looked on as a sort of intellectual bum.

So we began to go to parties all over town and sometimes even out in the country. This was a great achievement for both of us, because the snob thing in Dublin was, to my mind, stronger than it could have been anywhere else on earth. Anyway, I would go into my act and Redmond would stand around and spout his opinions about all kinds of things. And if anyone disagreed with him he was more than likely to turn round and tell them to 'get stuffed' or to 'shit and fall back in it', and he was considered to be 'a terrible character', which was praise indeed. It was the sort of thing that he was likely to say rather than what he was talking about that attracted people, and he knew it and he never let them down.

I found myself that even when I wasn't doing a turn I was still acting. Everything that I said was intended as entertainment. Every line was a gag, and the one that got a laugh was used again and again on different people. I couldn't help it. I wanted so badly to be on a stage that I was, even when I wasn't.

There was no shortage of women at the parties, but for the first time in years I wasn't all that bothered about sex. I had the stage in my mind and I had drinking in my blood, and apart from Breeda I hardly bothered doing any chasing at all. And I began to think that I was growing up.

It wasn't that I was going off women or anything like that. I still went a bit dry in the throat at the sight of strong legs and big breasts. It was just that sex was becoming a part of my life now, instead of being my whole life. Like most other changes that had taken place in me it happened without me being really conscious of it. You don't notice your pubic hairs until you see the bush.

At the same time Redmond was going through them, all over the place, and if he didn't find a masochist with money at least he found women who were far from penniless. And not one of them was under the impression that variation on a theme was a greyhound.

At a Sunday-night party in Skerries, north of Dublin, a man-eating American divorcee, who just loved 'this li'l ole country', took a real tumble for him. I wasn't surprised. With his crooked mouth and his Bohemian act he was bound to be a sensation, but he couldn't get over her very direct approach. 'She doesn't feck about, that one doesn't,' he said to me while she was at the lavatory. 'Told me she wanted me beside her when she woke up in the morning, and that I look pale and passionate, if you don't fuckin' mind.'

It was funny to see Redmond, the king of the all-time bullshit artists, puzzled by the way a woman talked to him, and I laughed for half a minute at the expression on his face.

'I'm glad you're amused,' he said. 'With friends like you, who needs bleedin' enemies?'

173

'Well, apart from the freckles you're definitely a paleface, and if you're not passionate by now you bloody well ought to be.'

'I wonder if she's got a lot of dough?' he said, half aloud.

'Well, she didn't get that jewellery she's wearing in Woolworth's, and that's for certain. Anyway, most Yanks that can afford to come over here usually are loaded. There's no harm in giving it a try. You might even win a talent contest.'

'You bastard. You sleeveen bastard,' he yelled into my face. 'You never won that clobber singing. I knew it, I just knew it.' And he started to laugh.

'It was a good yarn, though, wasn't it, Harry? Got you going, didn't it?'

He nodded, still laughing. 'You bleedin' liar. You're worse than me.'

The Yankee bird came back then and she stood at his elbow, smiling like a new bride. 'Oh, you're back. Hello. Uh, meet a fella who without doubt is the biggest bastardin' liar in creation. Paddy Maguire, eh, this is Mrs. Nichol from America.'

He winked at me. This was the way he talked to everyone, and instead of slinging him out on the lawn, as you might think they would, they loved it. She wasn't any different.

'Just call me Irenee.' She held out her hand and I shook it. 'May I call you Paddy?'

'You can call me what you like, darlin, as long as it's not too early in the morning.'

She laughed at that, despite its age, while Redmond mumbled something to the roof about 'Holy Jeysus'. Irenee was a fine-looking woman, with a large mouth and hot liquid eyes, and even if she was a bit flabby I couldn't see Redmond worrying about that. I mean, you could hardly stand up and say he was the most discriminating man in the world and expect to be taken seriously.

Irenee had a flat in town and she gave us both a lift back from Skerries. And it was obvious, without a word being said, that she wanted Redmond to spend the night with her, and if the way she drove that motor was anything to go by that highly sexed Yankee widow was going to give him a night to remember.

He phoned me next morning at the office and before I spoke to him I knew it must have been something important. He had never done that before and Redmond didn't get excited for nothing.

'Hello, Paddy. This is Harry.'

'Good morning. I'm surprised you're up so early. What's the matter?'

'What time do you get out to lunch?' he asked. 'Quarter to one?'

I said it was and he asked me to meet him in the Republican, which was a pub off Fleet Street. He didn't want to talk on the phone, so I said I'd see him. I couldn't wait for lunchtime to come. Whatever it was that had Redmond excited I wanted to hear about it.

He was drinking whiskey when I found him in the public bar and he had a double sitting on the counter for me. I didn't like whiskey that early in the day, but I drank it anyway while we waited for the pints of stout to come up.

'She wants to marry me,' he said, just like that, and he pulled a fiver out of his pocket to pay for the drinks.

'I hope you'll both be very happy,' I said, managing to keep my face straight.

'I mighta fuckin' known I'd get a lot of sympathy from you. I'm glad you think it's funny because I bleedin' well don't.'

I started to laugh and I couldn't stop it. The tears ran down my face and I got a pain in my ribs, and Redmond just stood there and waited patiently until I finally stopped. 'I'm sorry, Harry. Jeysus, I didn't mean to laugh. It's just the thoughts of you going to the altar.' I pulled my face straight again. 'Do you love her?'

'Look, you prick,' he said viciously. 'Save the jokes for your public. I'm in no mood for them.'

'Has she got money?'

'She's stacked,' he said. 'Gave me a score to buy myself some gear. I'm supposed to be going back there for lunch.'

'A score. Thank Jeysus for that. I haven't a pot.'

'Ah, well, that's one good thing. We can solve your financial problem.' He put his hand in his pocket and took out some notes He threw me three pounds. 'Right, now that I've paid you for your services, what in the name of Jeysus am I going to do?'

'Tell her you're a bumboy,' I said.

He didn't like that. For some reason he couldn't bear the idea of anyone thinking him homesexual. 'I will in me ballocks tell her I'm a queer. What do you take me for at all?'

'Well, marry her, then.'

'Don't be funny, Maguire. Anyway, after the number of times I sunk the log last night she'd never believe I was a brownie.'

'She might. Tell her you didn't want to hurt her feelings. Tell her you like her, tell her anything. She'll probably end up feeling sorry for you.'

'And what about the dough for the clobber? Give it back?'

'You're joking, aren't you? You'd only hurt her pride if you did that. No, buy some gear, show her you're not a bum.'

'I'm not a bum.'

'All right, I'll believe you. Don't you fancy her at all?'

' 'Course I fancy her. She's got money to burn and she doesn't mind spending it and she's red hot in bed. It's just that when they start on about wedding bells I want to get my gurcake and milk and get outa town.

'There's something else,' he said.

'What?'

'She wants to see some of my manuscripts.'

'Your manuscripts?'

'Yeh, my fuckin' manuscripts, and it's all your fault. All that ballocks in the car last night about me being a writer. You laid it on so thick that she believed every word you said.'

'Ah, for Jeysus' sake, Harry. She couldn't have.'

'I'm telling you she did. The way you went on she thinks she's found another James Joyce.'

I paid for two pints of Guinness, not knowing what to say to Redmond.

'She must be a right eejit,' I said finally.

'Brilliant,' he said. 'You worked that out all by yourself. Seriously, Maguire, what am I going to do about it?'

'Write something,' I said.

'Write something?'

'Yeh. Scribble down any crap that comes into your head. Anything at all. That's bound to take the heat out of her knickers.'

He looked at me as though I'd taken leave of my senses. 'Ah, come on now, Maguire. Cut the kiddin'. I'm nearly forty years of age and I've never even written a letter in my life.'

'All the better,' I said. 'It's bound to be so lousy that even an eejit like her will give you the bum's rush, and you won't have to tell her you're queer either.'

He liked that. A slow grin crept across his crooked mouth. and his eyes twinkled at the thought. 'Yeh, that's a real brain-wave, Maguire. You're welcome to the three nicker.' He stopped dead. 'But what'll l write about?'

'I'll say one thing for you, Redmond. You get your money's worth.' I took a drink and bit into the sandwich that was serving me as a lunch. 'Write about taking a scivvie up to The Dodder,' I said.

When I left him he went off to buy some lined foolscap and a pen and I walked up along College Green and I laughed all the way back to the office. During the afternoon tea break I told

Larry Deegan all about it and from that moment on Redmond had two of us waiting to hear the next bit of news.

In the evening I went into Campion's and Redmond wasn't there. I bought a drink, intending to leave after the one, but just then he came through the door and for a change it was my turn to wear the surprised look. This time it was Redmond who was wearing the new clobber and there was no two ways about it, he was a good-looking fella, in a funny kind of way.

He'd bought a blue double-breasted suit with a single button drape and he wore a light blue shirt and a silver tie. His hair had been cut and washed and he smelled like something out of a high-class knocking shop.

He sat down like a fella who'd just won the Sweepstake and he put a hole in my pint before he even said good evening. Then he put his right foot out so that I could see his plain black casual shoes, and I could only admire his taste.

'You'll have to come down with me, Maguire. That load of manure that I left with her at four o'clock. It was such rubbish. I can't face her on my own.'

I said all right. As far as I was concerned it was a right laugh, so after a few more pints we left the pub and hailed a taxi. When we got out of the car Redmond paid the fare and I knew that I was going to be sorry when he lost that sexy Yank.

Her flat was in Eglington Road, which was a fairly exclusive neighbourhood in those days. As I heard a fella say in a boozer one night, there wasn't a dog in town with enough courage to even piss up against a lamp-post in Eglington Road.

Irenee opened the door for us and we stepped into carpet that stopped somewhere in the location of the knee. She threw her arms around Redmond and they were kissing as if they were starving, and she looked so good in this pale pink dress that I could have given her one myself.

When she let him go for a breath she said hello to me and

made me very welcome. 'Excuse the state of the place, Paddy. I'm not really settled in yet.'

I looked around the lounge. Maybe it was in a state. I didn't know. I'd never been in a palace before. She went behind the bar and came up with a bottle of champagne and she poured three glasses.

'To Harry Redmond,' was her toast. 'To a great writer and a wonderful Irishman.'

Redmond and I looked at each other. We drank the champagne and we were both thinking she was a right nutter.

'I forgot to tell you,' Redmond said to me. 'This dame is not only a lustpot, she's a comedienne as well.'

She threw back her head and laughed, taking no notice of the fact that he'd called her a ragbag in well-chosen slang.

'You Irish. You're so modest it's almost a fault.'

'Look, for Jeysus' sake,' Redmond said to her. 'What are you blathering on about?'

'The story, Harry. Your beautiful story. It's poetry.'

'Now a joke's a joke, Irenee, but you know, don't go too far. A fella's only got so much patience.'

'It must be one of the ones I haven't read,' I said to her.

She finally realised that Redmond thought she was joking.

'Listen, Harry. Before I married my ex I was a newspaper woman, so don't try to tell me anything about writing. I was literary critic on five national newspapers.'

Redmond looked at me and he looked so puzzled that I felt really sorry for him. 'Give us a drink, for the lord's sake.'

Irenee filled the glasses again. 'Don't you think it's fantastic that such a talented person can be so off hand about his work, Paddy?'

'Yeh,' I said, 'oh, yeah. I'm always on at him about the same thing. He just doesn't listen.' I couldn't look at Redmond.

'And to think that he won't let anybody even read his work.

Why it's almost criminal.' She turned to Redmond. 'You've got no right to hide your talent. I won't allow you to go on doing it.'

Redmond looked angry, but she walked over to him and put her lips on his face. 'You crazy man. I'm in love with you.' I could feel myself blushing, as I sat there, because I knew she was serious. 'Do you think I'd make a monkey out of the man that I want to marry?'

He didn't answer her, but he turned to me. 'You and your bleedin' brainwaves,' he said helplessly.

'So it was you, Paddy. You persuaded him to let me see the story. I'm truly grateful to you.' She walked over and kissed me on the face and I knew for sure that she believed what she had been saying.

'May I read it, please? It's one I haven't seen.'

'Will you leave off, for Jeysus' sake,' Redmond yelled at me.

'I only want to read it.' I gave him a wink. 'What harm can that do?'

He nodded, getting my meaning. 'Yeh, okay. You read it.'

Irenee handed me the sheets of foolscap, then she took Redmond by the hand and they went into what could only be a bedroom. I sat down on a chair and the handwriting was about the best I've ever seen. Firm and bold, lying slightly to the right, and clear as print. The story was called 'My Lonely Love', and I wanted to laugh at the idea of Redmond sitting there trying to be all literary. But from the first two lines I didn't feel like laughing and it got me so much that I felt it was happening to me, right there and then.

It was about a fella giving one to a domestic servant and it was about every fella who ever did. While he was with her in the long grass he loved her and he told her so, and at the time he meant the words that poured out of him. Then, when the sex was finished and he let her go home alone, he hated himself for being such a bastard, but still he let her go. And he was sorry about that. He wanted to go after her and say good night to her in a gentle voice, but he didn't have the guts to get that much involved. And he suffered at his lack of guts, and he told stories about it to the fellas in the pub, and everybody laughed and told him he was a great character altogether, but he never laughed himself, not once.

That was the story, and to be fair it wasn't too badly written. But, God, I couldn't for the life of me see what Irenee was going on about. It was just another short story, and if it had any literary merit, well, I couldn't see it.

I sat there a while, trying to make up my mind about Irenee. She was either some kind of a nut or just so much in love with Redmond that she couldn't see the muck-heap for the flies.

They came back into the room and I didn't give a second thought to what they'd been doing. I was too busy trying to think of what to say. She looked at me expectantly. She wanted my opinion and she was hoping that I was going to back her up. At the same time Redmond wanted me to shoot the story down as hard as I could.

'It's a good story,' I said. Redmond bristled a bit and I winked at him. 'I'm not saying it's perfect or anything, Harry, but you certainly can write.'

He turned to Irenee. 'Could you make us a sandwich or something, darlin'?'

'Why, sure, gee, I'm sorry. I didn't think of it. I was so excited by the story that I clean forgot.'

'Ah, that's all right, but go on and do it now before you forget again.'

She smiled at me and went out of the room. 'What're you on about?' Harry asked me angrily.

'Listen,' I said. 'She's a nutter, so let her give herself a good time with the story. You don't want to blow her out and her loaded with dough. Now, do you?'

He thought about that for a second or two. 'No, not really I don't. But what if she keeps on at me to write more stuff?'

'Honest to God, Harry, I don't know what you're so worried about. As long as she finds you beside her in the bed when she wakes up in the mornings she won't fret too much about anything else. Anyway, you can always say you'll do it tomorrow, and then tomorrow you can say you'll do it the next day. It shouldn't be any problem for a bullshit artist like you. And I'll tell you this, if you sling her in just because she thinks you're a genius you're as big a bloody nutter as she is.'

'You're right,' he said, 'I know you are. It's just that she makes me feel tied down. I'm not used to that kind of thing.'

'Well, get used to it and stop talking rubbish. You'll never get another chance like this as long as you live. Jeysus, it's like winning the Irish Sweepstake!'

He nodded, agreeing with me despite himself. 'Okay, I'll play along and see how it goes.'

He went to live with her just after that and they seemed happy enough together. For a little while they had a bit of trouble with his mother. She kept appearing at the door with a priest, trying to get him back home. But Irenee saw to it that she got a nice few quid every Friday and they had no more bother from the oul' one after that. And I did all right as well. Two nights a week I saw Redmond and it was a marvellous change to have him buying the drink.

Meanwhile, I was choking to death in the office. I tried hard to do the work properly, but my complete lack of interest must have been obvious to anyone with a pair of eyes in his head. But nobody passed any remarks, so I just got on with it and didn't worry.

I had problems, though, trying to find a way to tell Ma that I was going to get away before very long. Every day she asked me if I was all right, but I couldn't take it as a cue to tell her that everything was all wrong. I tried, God knows I did, but the words wouldn't come, so I ambled through my daily routine, hoping for some kind of inspiration that never turned up.

The singing at night kept me from going mad. It was at least a taste of what I wanted most, but I missed Redmond standing at the back, winking his eye at me to let me know I was doing well. I was probably jealous too, thinking of him sitting somewhere nice, drinking champagne or something with his double-rich Yank. But I couldn't help liking the bastard. Imagine getting attached to a layabout like that! Doesn't seem possible when you think about it.

It was the sleeveen grin that I missed most, the crooked mouth and the dry wit that had been my schoolbook. And the obscene tongue that never failed to make me laugh, and the endless stories, mostly lies, that he told as though they were the gospel truth.

He never mentioned anything to me about going to America. Irenee told me during a party at her flat. She had to return home and Harry was going too. They both felt that he would be able to get down to his writing over in the States. The change of environment would stimulate his talent, she said. I agreed with her, wishing that it was me going instead of Redmond.

He didn't talk much about it in the weeks before they left and he wouldn't let me see them off. Irenee came into the office on the morning they were going, and when we kissed goodbye she handed me a note from Harry. I went back to my desk and when I sat down I opened the envelope. There was a five-pound note in it, which as it happens was a godsend, and there were six words printed on the postcard: 'Sing "Patsy Fagan" for me sometime.'

I knew that had to be a gag. Redmond didn't like Irish songs and he wasn't the least bit sentimental. At least, I was sure he wasn't.

I sat there thinking about him and all the things we'd done

together, and I knew that he had been a really big part of my life. Cahill came up and stood by my desk. I looked up at him and he threw a file down in front of me. 'I want an assessor out to those people not later then this afternoon.'

'Yes, sir,' I said. 'I'll see to it right away.'

16

DURING the couple of months following Redmond's departure I drank more than ever. I even started knocking them back at lunchtime, which was something I'd rarely done before. This made the afternoons in the office double hard, and a couple of times I was so high that I still don't know how I got away with it. In the evenings I drank in the singing houses, but I never went to Campion's again.

I still saw Breeda, but the steam had gone out of it for me. She didn't seem to notice it, but then she was usually drunk before she had sex. Even the odd things that she liked so much to do didn't excite me the way they had done for so long. And as we drifted away from each other I began to have a nibble here and there, and being a bit of a singer made it easy. Entertainers draw women like a manure-heap does flies.

Redmond never wrote to me, but Irenee dropped me the odd line. He was going to start writing any day now, and they were still together. But the fact that she never mentioned drink left me thinking that he was pissing it up. And since he'd left his mother had become a right 'Red Biddy' drinker. Whatever money Redmond sent her went on plonk, and she was footless every time you saw her. She was one oul' one that I'd never had much time for. A miserable calculating oul' bitch she'd always been, but during the time that she was drinking herself to death she was a nice happy old soak and you couldn't help liking her. Like most of the women on The Hill she'd had very little out of life. But I'll tell you one thing, when Mrs. Redmond got the chance she took it with both hands, and I can't ever remember seeing an oul' one die as happy as she did. An oul' fella named Gill, who had knocked about with her since she'd come into the few quid from Harry, told me that she died on her back, singing a dirty song, but he was such a filthy, sleeveen of a man that I just couldn't believe him. I know that 'Red Biddy' drinkers do some desperate things by times, but that seemed a bit strong to me.

The funny thing was that neither Mrs. Redmond or my own mother knew anything about my connection with Redmond. I'd never mentioned him at home and Redmond had hardly ever spoken to his old lady, except to tell her to get out of his road or something like that.

I began to get more one-night stands with the little dance band, and though I gave Ma half of everything I earned I knew that she wasn't keen on me singing. It was too uncertain to Ma's way of thinking. Not having had security she thought it was the most important thing in life. But I didn't discuss it with her, knowing that it wouldn't do any good.

Most nights it was after twelve when I got into bed, so I gave up the paper round. I didn't say anything to the people in the shop. I just stopped going and that was something else that caused a bit of bad feeling between Ma and me. It wasn't fair, she said. The people were entitled to notice so that they could find someone else to take my place. I didn't argue, though I felt like telling her to shut up. I didn't feel any obligation to anyone, least of all to people who paid ten bob for six mornings work, winter and summer.

I began to find it hard to get out of bed in the mornings and that was what started Ma on at me about the drinking. She knew to look at me when I finally got out of bed that I'd had a skinful the night before, and sometimes she didn't talk to me for days on end. The saddest part of all this was that I didn't care. For so long I'd worried myself sick in case I ever hurt Ma. Now I did what I wanted to do and if she felt hurt as a result I thought to myself that it was just too bad.

The one-night stands were great experience for me and I soon learned to pace myself for an evening's singing without ending up with laryngitis. And the practice killed any nerves that I'd had, so that I really felt right for the chance that I felt had to come sooner or later.

Every day I bought *The Irish Independent* and I went straight to the stage column. For months there was nothing of interest to me but I felt that it was there I'd find my chance really to get into show business.

It was at this time that Breeda and I broke up for keeps. I'd had enough and I liked her so much that I told her out straight, thinking that she was the one woman who would understand. It was the first time in my life that I'd ever been honest with a woman. If I'd let her down a few times or got so drunk that I couldn't perform she'd have given me the push, but when I told her she went berserk and when I tried to reason with her she attacked me. As true as God, she tried to stick me with a pair of scissors, and she was so strong that I had to punch the bejeysus out of her before she passed out. It was funny, in a way. That was the first evening I'd ever hit her with all my heart and soul, and I think that for once she didn't get any pleasure out of it.

I told Larry about it and I think he was a bit wary about seeing too much of her after that. He was a full-time inspector now, so I didn't see him as often as before, but we drank together whenever we could and it was only his encouragement to wait for the right moment that kept me in the office so long.

When I saw the advert in *The Independent* I knew it was the one I'd been waiting for, and as I wrote the letter for the job I was sure that I would get it. For once it wasn't ego that made me feel like that, I just felt it was fate.

187

A few days later I got a phone call at the office, and when I said hello the fella at the other end told me he was ringing about my answer to his advertisement. It had been for a vocalist who would be willing to play parts with a repertory and variety show that toured small towns all over Ireland.

'My name is Jimmy Frazer. I'd like to meet you for a chat.'

I was thrilled that I'd gotten this far. The photograph I'd sent had been a good one and I knew that if I could get talking to him, and maybe do a song or two, I'd be away in a hack. So, I arranged to meet him in Feeney's boozer, which was the pub where Redmond had taken me the night he conned me into singing for the first time. I was well known there, and Johnnie the pianist would help me all he could.

I didn't go home from work. I was a bit nervous and if Ma saw that she'd start asking questions and I didn't feel like being cross-examined. Instead I had a few pints and a sandwich, while I sat and worked out my patter and what numbers I was going to do. That kept me busy, and it was only when I got up on the bike to cycle across town to Feeney's that I thought about this chance to get away from The Hill.

Jimmy Frazer was a complete stranger to me and we hadn't talked much on the phone. You had to be careful with that O'Boyle listening in all the time. He'd sounded like a reasonable fella, though, and the fact that I was working in an office and wasn't a full-time professional hadn't seemed to bother him. And I felt that this was a good omen.

I had to wait for a half-hour in Feeney's lounge before Johnnie the pianist arrived. I told him what I wanted and he gave me a run-through a couple of numbers and said he'd give me a bit of *ad lib* music for my patter. I bought him a drink then and we sat and chatted until Jimmy Frazer arrived.

Although I hadn't seen him before I knew who he was the minute he came into the lounge. He had showman written all over him and when I stood up he came over to me with a grin on his face. He was a big man with a smooth handsome face and he looked like a straight fella.

We shook hands and I bought a round of drinks. He told me that he ran a small touring show and that he needed a singer who could also play parts in drama. And he told me right off that my appearance was just what he'd hoped it would be, and that provided I could put over a number I was in.

I sang 'The Birth of the Blues' and Johnnie really helped me on the piano. I was singing well. I could feel it, and though there weren't many people in the lounge I got a great hand when I finished. Then I did a few minutes' patter that had them all laughing well, and when I finished up with 'Patsy Fagan' I felt that I had done a really good turn. I thought of Redmond then and I wondered how he was doing over in the States. Even this lounge, which was one of my favourites, didn't seem the same without him, and his mouth on him like a torn pocket standing looking at me.

When I sat down again Jimmy Frazer told me that the job was mine if I wanted it. I was thrilled, and we shook hands on it and had another drink. I made arrangements to join the show in County Meath, on the following Monday week, and he agreed to wire me confirmation of his offer. I asked him to send it to the office because when Ma found out about this I had to break it to her in my own way, though right then I wasn't all that sure how that was going to be.

From that night on I was in a terrible state of nerves, because now that the thing had happened I was faced with the prospect of giving a week's notice in the job, as well as having to tell Ma. And I didn't fancy facing Mr. Hayes with the news, not after all the effort he'd put into me.

The telegram arrived just before Friday at lunchtime and I went and had a drink as soon as I got out of the office. I needed a few if I was going to go home and tell Ma. But I didn't go home. I just sat there drinking, not able to find the guts to get off the stool.

I had a very busy afternoon in the office and I was glad of that, telling myself that I'd talk to Mr. Hayes in the morning. After work I went straight home. It was no good putting it off any longer. Ma had to be told, and the longer I left it the harder it was becoming to face it.

'You've done what?' She turned from the gas stove and there was a bite in her voice that I'd never heard her use except to the oul' fella.

'I've taken a job in show business. I'm supposed to start on Monday week.' The words jumped out of my mouth. It was one time when my funny-man façade wasn't any good to me.

'You're not going. You're not leaving that job. I won't let you be so bloody foolish.'

Her eyes were full of tears from the effort she was making to control her temper and it was the first time she'd ever sworn at me.

'Ma, listen. It's something I want to do.'

'I will not listen!' she screamed at me and put the pan down so hard that chips fell all over the floor. 'I will not listen to you. But you just listen to me.' She was shaking with temper. 'I've stood by and let you do what you liked, and if this is the result may God forgive me for it. You've become a drunken young pup.' Her words were like blows in the face. 'An oul' man before your time, but by God you'll listen to me now! You'll listen and you'll do as I say.'

'Ma——'

'Shut up!' she screamed. 'God blast you, shut up!'

She sank on to a chair and she was shaking so much and her face was so white that I thought she was going to pass out. I reached across the table, trying to take her hand, but she pulled away from me with such force that cups were smashing to the floor.

'I've got to go, Ma. I've got to get away from here.'

'You won't leave that job. I won't let you ruin your life.

You bloody young fool, I've watched my own life dry up because I followed my heart, and that's just what you're doing. You're too young to know your own mind.'

'I know what I want, Ma, and it's not an office job for the rest of my life.'

She began to sob and her body shook from the force and my insides twisted at the sound. It was useless trying to reason with her. She was twenty times more stubborn than I was.

'I don't want to hurt you, Ma, but I'm going. I've got to.'

She looked at me, and if it was possible for her to hate me she did at that moment. Her eyes were flat with anger, like they'd been the time the oul' fella was going to hit Larry for coughing.

'I'd sooner see you dead at my feet first.'

The words were cold now and she chilled me with the sound of her voice. I held back my tears. 'Ma, be fair. I've always tried to help you. For as long as I can remember, I've tried. Now I've just got to think of myself.'

'Help me! Help me!' she hissed. 'Oh God, you're a great one altogether, aren't you? With your few bob when you were up to something that you knew wasn't right. God, Paddy, you must think I'm awful stupid. Like the two pound you gave me when you told that cock-and-bull story about the suit that you brought back from your holiday, and you with pucks of money in your pocket. It's an awful pity someone hasn't given you a medal.'

I didn't say anything. I suppose she must have gone down my pockets. That was something I'd never have expected of her. But that didn't hurt me as much as knowing I'd been caught out on a lie.

'I don't know where you got the stuff and I don't know where you got the money and I don't care a damn.' She stood up and she began to cry again. 'Go and do what you like. Go to hell for all I care, but listen to me, mister. You leave that job and you'll never darken this floor again. As God is my judge I'll never speak to you again, not as long as there's a breath in my body. And that's my final word to you.'

She turned her back on me and I knew there wasn't anything I could do for her.

'I'm sorry, Ma,' I said. 'I love you as I've always done.'

I stood up from the table and I went out on to the street, not seeing where I was going for the scalding tears that hurt my eyes.

She'd understand someday. Someday she'd forgive me for hurting her so. She was my mother and she knew that I loved her. Sometime she'd know that I left her because I had to get up and go.

I drank whiskey in Ranelagh and nothing was further from my mind than Jimmy Frazer and my promise to him to join his show. Just then I wanted nothing more than to move. To go somewhere and to just keep on going.

When I got off the bus at Dunlaoghaire I was cold and my insides were numb from the shock of Ma's words. People who get hurt easily have the power to hurt others, more than they know. As long as I lived I'd never forget the way she looked at me that evening.

I bought a ticket for Holyhead, and as I went up the gang-plank I realised that I didn't have so much as a clean shirt under my arm. But the thought went as quickly as it had come, and in a few minutes I was drinking from the small bottle that I'd brought with me. But I knew that if I drank a gallon I would still feel cold inside.

I watched the lights of the harbour slide away from the old mail-boat and the sad part was that I felt nothing. I was alone on the upper deck. I was a part of the night, like a shadow standing among shadows.